DANGEROUS TIES

A
TIES
NOVEL
#1

J.L. BECK

Love,
J.L.
Beck
xoxo

Editing and Interior Design: Silla Webb
Alpha Queens Book Obsession- Author Services
Cover Design by Sprinkles on Top
Stock Photography by Dollar Photo Club
© JL Beck 2016

Dangerous Ties by J.L. Beck

DEDICATION

For Tonya; this book belongs to you. Like a rose beyond a wall,
may you forever bloom.
Rest in peace.

A rose once grew where all could see,
sheltered beside a garden wall,
And as the days passed swiftly by,
it spread its branches, straight and tall...
One day, a beam of light shone through
a crevice that had opened wide
The rose bent gently toward its warmth
then passed beyond to the other side
Now, you who deeply feel its loss,
be comforted – the rose blooms there-
its beauty even greater now
-   A.L. Frink

ABOUT THE AUTHOR

J.L. Beck is the bestselling author of numerous books including Indebted, Inevitable, Invincible, and The Bittersweet Series. She's best known for weaving a tale, that ends with your mouth hanging open, and your hands gripping the edge of your seat.

She's a no holds bar author who enjoys spending time with her husband of eight years, three-year-old hellion, and soon to be newborn son Kolden, as well as Hatchi & Halo her two fur babies. She calls Wisconsin home, but loves to travel. In her free time you can catch her watching bad reality tv, cooking, reading books, or spending time outdoors.

Links:

FB: @J.L. Beck
Twitter: @AuthorJLBeck
IG: @AuthorJLBeck
Sign up for updates: http://eepurl.com/2aydr

ACKNOWLEDGMENTS

First off I need to thank my fans. I know it has been hard waiting months upon months for me to release a book. Pregnancy hasn't been easy on me and makes writing let alone doing anything else almost impossible. Therefore, thank you for sticking by me through all of this. You're the best fans ever.

Secondly is my marketing team, my pimper's, my two PA's, along with the numerous bloggers that have helped me. Thank you for putting up with me and all the changes I have had to make. I'm surprised some of ya'll haven't attempted to ring my neck yet.

Hubs. You mean a lot to me. Thanks for trying to deal with all my emotions.

Bella. Your questions keep me sane.

Kolden. Thanks for waiting long enough for me to finish this book.

Psss.. please leave a review once finished

ONE

I knew the moment I laid eyes on her I had to have her. My body hummed with energy, my muscles tightened with tension, and my cock grew thick with anticipation of hitting the bottom of her stroke after stroke.

"Grayson," Tuck's deep voice said my name with inquisition. He must've seen that my attention was elsewhere, that something or rather someone had caught my eye long enough to distract me from him. I laughed a little to myself, Tuck was always making sure we stuck to any plan we came up with, so going off script right now had his attention fully on me.

I ran a hand through my thick hair and then down my face. It had been months since my last adventure outside of anything that didn't include knives, death, or blood being spilled across a concrete floor.

"Tucker," I said his name with the same tone, my eyes meeting his dark ones. His thick eyebrows shot up, and a smooth smirk spread across his arrogant face.

Tuck was a handsome fucker with his dirty blonde hair and forrest green eyes, but there was more to him than his good looks. His body was built for the kill, his mind sharp as a nail, and his dominant nature always in full effect.

Then there was me. Being a killer wasn't by choice. When your parents' owed money to someone and payment was late, something was taken in return. Something or someone. That someone was me. Boss took me and made me into exactly what he saw fit. A murderer is what I became. I dealt with the death and blood that loomed around me the only way I knew how.

I relished in it. And if your name ended up on my list, you were good as dead. After all, I had a vengeance—a thirsty need for blood that couldn't be quenched no matter how many times I slaughtered those that took from me. Then things changed. I changed.

Sometimes you were just the pawn in the middle of a war bigger than you ever suspected.

Secrets of the past were exposed, sides were taken, and it was then that I realized loyalty was not given freely but earned. Especially when it was your family at risk.

A menacing growl escaped Tuck's mouth, pulling me from my own fucked up thoughts. My eyes immediately met the cold stare in his. He knew I wasn't fucking around tonight, no matter what the fuck he had to say about it. When I went back to the seedy hotel room I was currently occupying, I wasn't going back alone.

"She's too pretty, too—" Tuck paused for a moment as I turned my attention back to her.

"Too goody to shoes, if you know what I mean." He leaned in close to me, the whiskey on his breath permeating the air. I was used to it by now, though. I understood the need to drink to cover up all the chaos you found yourself intertwined with each day.

Taking a deep breath, I eyed her from my seat. Music blared and lights flashed around us while sweaty bodies rubbed against one another. Clubs really weren't our thing, but when we finally found a moment to ourselves that didn't revolve around the art of torture, we decided we'd come to the club a couple blocks over to unwind, find an easy target to do in the toilet, and get some fucking relief. But, of course, I would throw caution to the wind the moment I spotted someone out of my league.

I cracked my knuckles, my body was wired up, but it wasn't because of the things going on around me. Nah, it had everything to do with the piece of hot ass across the room. I smiled, knowing that I was going in for the kill and there was no way of escaping me.

Dangerous Ties by J.L. Beck

"The good ones always fall the hardest for the bad boys." I shot him a smirk, downing the rest of my jack and coke. I wasn't really ready to get up and converse with anyone, I was more ready to slam balls deep into someone and listen to the sound of our skin smacking against one another's. I guess conversation was a good place to start, though, shoving your dick in just any hole that was open could leave you with more than one problem.

"Good luck, Gray." Tuck laughed, giving up on his attempt to keep me at bay. Instead, I watched him push from our table and walk over to a corner booth, a wide smile forming on his lips as he came to a standstill in front of a woman with bleach blonde hair and tits just as fake as everything else on her. They exchanged words and then he was sliding in beside her and pulling her from her cushioned seat into his lap. The woman threw her head back laughing loudly as she wrapped an arm around Tuck's neck. I chuckled lightly to myself, he always went for the loud ones. The attention whores. The ones who begged for you to fuck them harder, but then cried later on when you gave them everything they asked for.

Getting up from the booth, my boots felt heavy against the sleek flooring. I didn't fit in here, if anything I stuck out like a sore fucking thumb. I was wearing a pair of dark jeans, a white t-shirt I planned on getting covered in blood later, and my lucky leather jacket. I didn't use any cologne, nor did I style my hair like so many other jackoffs in this place did. Who fucking needed that shit anyway?

"Hey..." A sultry voice mumbled off to my right. I rolled my eyes as I caught glimpse of her makeup covered face and kept walking, not even giving her the attention that she desperately craved. I was desperate for some action, that was true, but I also knew what I liked and what I didn't. I wasn't about to entertain the first woman who threw herself at me. Even the world's most deadly killers had standards.

My eyes quickly circled the room, from the floor to the top of the stairs and then back down again. The place was packed and smelt of sweat, sex, and alcohol. I could feel eyes on me, and immediately I honed in on whom it was that was staring me down from across the room.

She had long, dark hair that was pulled back in a *pull-my-hair-fuck-me* kind of way. The dress that encased her hot little body was dark, her eyes a midnight blue that reminded me of the ocean. Staring into them, I could feel a wave of uneasiness wash over me. She was going to be trouble with a motherfucking capital T. Without further hesitation, I made my way over to her reminding myself that I was here to get some good sex, drink a few cold ones, and kill some fuckers that deserved it when the time arose. That was all.

I pushed through the masses of bodies, making my way to the front of the club where the bar and the mystery woman were located. My cock jutted to the beat of the music as my blood pounded in my ears. I was a lion on my first hunt, the prey within sight. All I had to do was sink my teeth into her.

I turned my attention to the bar, hoping to order another drink when I felt someone watching me.

"Hey there, killer..." I turned just in time, taking notice of just how beautiful she was. Her skin was as white as the snow on a winter morning, making the blue of her eyes pop out that much more. Her hair was dark like I had first noticed, but had dark flecks of red in it, too. She was lean, but slightly shapely in the hips, perfect for gripping and slamming into.

I watched her eyes zero in on my mouth as my tongue flicked out onto my bottom lip. I could see the lustful-haze fill them. She didn't have to say a word, not even speak her name. I knew she wanted me, simply by the way she rubbed her legs together, and by the way she looked at me as if I was a glass of water on the hottest day in July.

"Tell me your name, then I'll buy you a drink and we can be on our way." I bent down whispering into her ear. I could feel her pulse jump, thrumming loudly in her throat, as if it was beating loudly in my ears. Her eyes grew big with apprehension, as if she wasn't sure she wanted to do such a thing.

"Ellie Goodwin." This time when she spoke it was much softer, much more quiet in comparison to the girl who had just addressed me a moment ago.

Dangerous Ties by J.L. Beck

"Well, Ellie, what do you want to drink?" I smiled, not wanting to frighten her away. At least not yet. I would save that for when I was done having my way with her.

She pursed her lips and tilted her head at me as if she was making an internal decision. I knew these things. I could read people like the back of my hand. When a lie was forming in their mind, I was already pulling the trigger on my gun.

"Straight whiskey please." As she spoke, I could feel the courage coming back into her words. It caused a smile to form upon my face. One that I just couldn't hide. I told the order to the bartender and watched him make our drinks right before us.

"I saw you watching me. Did you know staring is rude?" I questioned, allowing the previous smile to linger against my lips.

"You stared first, I was just following suit." Ellie bit at her bottom lip, lifting her glass to take a drink. I loved the smartass mockery that came from her mouth, it made me want to do very bad fucking things to her body.

"Anyone ever tell you that following someone else's lead almost always leads you down a dangerous road?" I leaned into her body, feeling her warmth surround me and her smell invade my senses.

Her eyes twinkled in the shitty club lighting, it was as if she wanted to be in danger, as if she craved it. A moment of silence lingered between us. I watched curiously as she downed the rest of her drink and then she leaned into my body, her breasts pushing against my chest.

"The dangerous road is always the less traveled road, and let's just say I'm looking for something with no traffic jams." She smiled, all her white teeth showing.

Looking at her, I knew she had no idea what she was talking about. She was exactly what Tuck had called her, a good girl. She probably had a mommy and daddy who paid for all of her shit. Friends and family who would miss her if she ever went missing.

"What you're getting tonight is going to be as close to the dangerous side of life as you can get." I flashed my teeth at her, a warning tone in my voice. Ellie's blue eyes grew darker and bigger as if she was imagining just what it was I had meant. Just as she sat her glass down, I grabbed her hand, pulling her from the stool she was sitting on.

"Where are we going?" she asked from behind me, her nervous tone reaching my ear as I weaved us through the crowd towards the exit door. I didn't have to give her an answer. I didn't have to say anything. The moment she accepted my drink was the moment she had given herself to me for one night. I didn't need to explain things to her, but for her, because she seemed so perfect, so wrong for me I would.

"I'm going to take you back to my hotel. Fuck you. Then leave you there while the lingering feeling of my cock being inside of you wears off. After that you can run along and tell all your friends what it was like to have sex with one of the most dangerous men in New York." I growled pushing through the back door. I didn't even bother to look over my shoulder and see the shocked look stuck on her face

ELLIE

TWO

My stomach twisted in knots as his sweaty palm rested against mine. The cold wind against my skin was a relief as we barreled through the back door of the club. Darkness surrounded us, all exceptt for the small light post at the end of the alleyway which did nothing but cast a small shadow around us. I knew coming here was a mistake, I never stepped outside my comfort zone. It could lead to being caught, and I promised myself that would never happen. I wouldn't become a victim again.

My chest heaved, but I still felt as if I couldn't breathe. I wasn't living, just working and coming home. I was playing it safe. I was a suffocating mess at the end of every single day.

"There's no turning back, Ellie. No saying no…" I shook my head, trying to figure out if this was a dream or not. Had I actually gotten myself into this mess? Had I attempted to be strong and courageous for the first time in my life, even more so to a man that I didn't even know the name of.

"What did you say your name was again?" I tried to sound nonchalant about it, but I couldn't hide the tone in my voice. He stopped mid-step, his boots crunching against the rocks beneath his feet. He swiveled around, forcing our bodies to clash against one another. Every single place his skin touched mine, fire sparked. It was as if he was gasoline, and I was the match needed to start the fire.

"I didn't… but it's Grayson." The way his name slid off his tongue caused my head to spin, every word that fell from his lips was thick and heavy with lust as he stared into my eyes. He was so much more up close than I had expected. Tall, dark, and dangerous in the best way. His eyes bled into my soul, reading my every thought. A sharp chin that was covered with a full dark beard, one you couldn't help but want to grab and pull.

Knowing that these thoughts would get me nowhere, I shook my head. As much as I felt a pull towards him, I could see warning signs all around him cautioning me away. Why? I didn't know, especially now when he seemed calm, cool, and collective. As if telling me he was one of New York's most dangerous men was nothing but a reason to try and push me away.

"Gray..." His name wasn't even spoken from my lips fully, and I was being picked up and slammed against the brick wall behind me. The harshness of the bricks against my skin as my shirt rode up, the slight pain that radiated through my head from the impact made me question my decision to talk to this man. Yet, I was unable to focus on anything but him the second his firm lips came down upon my own.

A breath heaved in my chest, stilling everything around me for one moment. Grayson kissed me like he was on a mission, like a man starved of love and affection his entire life. My hands instinctively fell to his shoulders, my nails digging into the leather of his jacket. His smell fell over me, consuming me. It was one of darkness and rain. As if he was a thunderstorm barreling down the Nebraska grasslands.

"Mmmm..." he mumbled against my lips as he bit at them tenderly, begging for me to give him more. Slowly, I did so, our tongues becoming one as we mingled together. Every inch of my body was pressed against his, my breast flushed against his chest, thighs tightly clenched around his waist, and my fingers sinking deeply into the crooks of his shoulder blades. My body temperature was rising, my pussy dripping with a need I had never felt before. It had been months since I last had sex, and given the situation I was in there was a very good reason as to why. I mean it was hard to find someone when you were supposed to be in hiding. Even harder when almost every man you found yourself attracted to, knew who your father was. But none of that mattered to me now; now I just wanted Grayson to

14

rip my clothes off right here and take me. Nothing else mattered in this moment but the way he made me feel as his hands roamed over my body.

"You're intoxicating." I wanted to scream the words but couldn't, my body refused to allow me, instead they came out like a whisper barely being heard over our pants. Grayson pulled away from me slowly, his eyes never leaving mine, a pure adulterated need that mirrored my own reflected back at me. I watched the desires of lust mingle and swirl with something else... something that I had never seen before. It was a cross between wanting something and the desire to actually keep it. It was as if he was used to never holding on long enough to something. He licked his lips, causing my stomach to flip.

"If I could keep one thing, keep one person in my life, even having just met you." He paused, looking both ways down the alleyway... As if someone would pop out at any second and attack him.

"It would be you." He finished. The look in his eyes told me his words couldn't be any more true. I gripped his shoulders tighter, understanding his words and the meaning behind them. We clearly had met by coincidence, but still it felt like our circumstances had fated us. Pulling his face into my own, I carefully watched him. My hands gliding underneath his shirt, making a trail over his abs and chest. Every inch of him was ripped, warm, and smooth. Without thought I bit my lip wanting to sink my teeth into his skin.

"Fucker! I said to leave me alone. You ain't got no shit on me." A deep voice sounded down the alleyway. It was loud and full of anger. It sounded as if someone was having an altercation, and altercations to me meant being found. Instinctively Grayson pulled away from me, but his grip grew tighter as his breaths became heavy and even in the dim lighting I could see the darkening of his once blue eyes, mixing with a stormy grey within a matter of seconds. Fear started to form in my belly as a shiver ran down my back. I started to go back revert back into my own memories, but the voice on the other end of the alleyway pulled me out of my own mind.

"Once a hit is established we come to collect, and by collect I do mean take your dead body to those who have placed the hit." A much deeper, menacing voice rang in my ears. I could sense the change in the air and in Grayson almost simultaneously.

He must've recognized the voice because he released me immediately as if he wasn't just about to rip my clothes off. He walked with a purpose in the direction of the two men. I stared in wonder for a moment, my body feeling as if it was on fire. Never in my entire life had someone sparked something in me like he did. Without another thought, I followed suit not wanting to be left behind, even if every fiber of who I was told me that I needed to run the opposite way.

"You expect me to believe that bullshit? Do you know who the fuck I am?" The voice grew louder as we approached. It was in the dim lighting that I saw a man in his late twenties standing against the wall of the business across the alley. He was dressed in a suit, his tie was red, and his hair was dark, slicked back in a way that said he felt highly of himself. One look at him and I could see he came from money and politics. A life I once knew all too well about. This was all too familiar for me, and I found myself being brought back to the past.

"Money cannot buy you happiness, Father!" I screamed the words at him. How was it that I understood this more than him? I knew what it was that he did, how he "helped" people win elections over and over again. He would never understand the meaning.

He smiled smugly, and my stomach jumped into my throat. "When you have it, it can buy you whatever you want. Just remember that..." My stomach churned knowing the dirty deeds he would have his men do.

I started to fall further into my own memories, but the voice on the other end of the alleyway pulled me from the past.

"Nice of you to show up, Grayson." A large burly man who stood across from the other man spoke harshly, his tone implied he was annoyed. Grayson tipped his chin up, his fists clenched in anger as he came to a halt beside the beastly man. I stood very still wondering what would happen next. My mind reeled with a million thoughts as I ran over what they had previously been talking about while I was further down the alley.

16

Dangerous Ties by J.L. Beck

"I'll take it from here, Tuck," Grayson said. I could feel the change in him taking over, the darkness settling into him. It caused a ripple of goosebumps to form against my skin. Grayson turned towards me just as his hand slithered under his jacket. Unsure of what it was that he was going to pull out, I instinctively took a step back. My blood began to move as if it had ice in it, panic almost seizing me as I saw the blade of a knife come into view.

"What about her?" Tuck gestured to me, his words smacking me right in the face. I hadn't realized just how out of place I truly fucking was.

"What about her? Are you kidding me? You fuckers think you'll get away with this? That the FBI and CIA won't come after you? My family has money, lots of it. They'll find you." The man against the wall didn't seem to be begging for his life, but more so threatening the man named Tuck and Grayson's lives. One would think you would be begging for your life, but I guess when you felt you had the upper hand you didn't really need to.

My life felt like it was hanging in the balance just like the man in the suit's life was. I was starting to regret ever meeting Grayson.

"Don't let her leave," Grayson growled, his eyes refusing to meet mine as I saw the murderous rage in them form. The man that had possessed my body in ways that were unimaginable just moments ago with a single kiss was gone. In his place was something that I had grown up with for the better part of my life.

A Killer. A monster. A man who understood death.

"If you kill me, they'll find you. They'll kill you. All of you," the man bellowed, puffs of his breath filled the air. Grayson seemed unfazed by his comments, taking another step forward. His boots were heavy, and even if I didn't want to watch what was about to happen I knew I had to.

Why, Ellie?

Because it would be the only reason I had not to sleep with him. Not to give myself up to him.

Grayson lifted the blade of his knife without a care. His movements were fast and precise, giving the man little chance to react. There was no confrontation, no screaming, just the silent gurgling of blood as it filled the man's throat, suffocating him.

My hands went straight to my mouth. I wouldn't scream, I never did. Not even when I watched my father kill my own mother. Instinct told me I needed to run.

A wave of nausea hit me, acid filling my throat as I watched the man slump over and eventually hit the ground. His body fell with a thud, echoing in the dark night. Grayson stood over the man for a short moment.

Tuck's eyes were on me, and I knew what he was doing. He was waiting, watching for the moment that I would run.

"What were the instructions?" Grayson's voice rattled in my ears. He sounded so uncaring, as if he hadn't just ripped life from someone. My body began to shake. After all I had done to remove myself from this type of life: the running, the hiding, the events and moments in my life I had missed because I was on the run. It all seemed to be following me, creeping it's way back in little by little.

"Pieces," Tuck answered, his eyes icing over as they met my own. The air around me grew heavy at the one word that left his mouth. *Pieces?* I knew what that meant even if I didn't want to think about it.

I clenched my fists together as tightly as I possibly could, attempting to stop the shaking that was racking my body. I channeled that little girl I had been all my life, and just as I saw Grayson slam the knife into the man's chest I knew that was my cue. I wanted Grayson, but I wanted my freedom from this life so much more.

Without a thought of what could go wrong, I did exactly what they expected of me. I ran. Every breath that fell from my lips was a pant, my legs burned from overuse as my feet pounded against the ground, and I ran with all my might down the alleyway towards the only exit. Panic seized me as my body pushed through the pain. I could hear the loud thud of boots and voices behind me, but I refused to stop, I couldn't because stopping meant death.

"Stop or I'll shoot you." I heard Tuck yell in my direction, but I continued running. He could shoot me. I had been shot before, it wasn't a big deal to me. I just wanted to escape, to run, and never look back on this moment again.

When I didn't hear the sound of a bullet being shot I was relieved, but that relief only lasted for a minute. Just as I reached the end of the alleyway, a heavy body landed against mine forcing me to the ground and all the air from my chest. My knees scraped against the unforgiving concrete, and the sound of fabric ripping filled the air.

"Running just gets you killed, didn't I tell you I was one of the most dangerous men in New York." Grayson's voice was filled with anger, the weight of his body against mine almost suffocating.

Just like that I knew I had been caught, like an animal in a snare I had become the prey once again. Before I could even muster up a response to what he had said, an arm was being wrapped around my throat. Panic took over as it tightened, the muscles in my body filling with fire as I tried to fight the inevitable.

"Don't fight me, Ellie." His tone was a demand as his muscles grew tighter around my airway. Trying to swallow, my throat felt dry and my tongue was heavy as I fought against his weight knowing my time was ticking away. Yet, as my body scraped against the rocks and a sheen of sweat formed on my body, I knew that I had all but lost the battle. Air refused to enter my lungs no matter how hard I fought against his hold.

"If you keep fighting me I will just kill you, and I don't want to have to kill you…" His word lingered, "…yet." I could barely make out what it was that he was saying. My eyes continued to grow heavy, and my heartbeat pounded in my ears. As much as I didn't want to give in to the blackness, I knew there was no other option. At least in the darkness I was safe.

Right?

THREE

Frustration poured from me as I made my way to our blacked out SUV. Ellie's breaths were heavy in my ears as I rolled her body into the back of the truck. I had no other option but to take her, and honestly I didn't want one.

While I tackled Ellie to the ground Tuck had finished the job, doing all the dirty work. I wanted nothing more than to get laid tonight but had somehow ended up getting my hands dirty, collecting a debt, and having to kidnap a woman because they were now a witness to a fucking murder.

"If you had just killed her, then you wouldn't have a reason to be frustrated, now would you?" Tuck's annoying voice was getting on my last fucking nerve.

"Funny. Opinions are like assholes, everyone has one," I said, irritated beyond disbelief while Tuck's laughter filled the SUV. After I secured her in the back of the truck by tying her hands and feet together and gagging her, I went back to help him load the pieces into a bag. We placed the body bag in the back seat and jumped into the truck, taking off.

I had just managed to get into the driver's seat once again after dropping the bag off at the location that was stated on the statement. As I slid the key into the ignition, my eyes caught on my hands. They were still coated in dry blood.

"Where are we going now? I'm not sure that we can take her back to the house," Tuck added, pulling me from my thoughts. I knew he was right. Bringing her back to the house would cause more trouble and eventually would lead to her

20

death. The other men didn't have women there. There was no reason to. That's what cheap hotels and clubs like the one we had been at were for.

"I don't fucking know, Tuck. This is about as far as I got with my thinking," I admitted out loud, beating my hand against the steering wheel as if a better answer would pop into my head from the act of rage.

You shouldn't have fucking ran after her. You should've let Tuck shoot her. Kill her in cold blood.

I was fighting against my inner demons, the part of me that wanted to kill her and throw her body in the Manhattan River. Yet, here she sat in the back of my fucking SUV, bound and gagged, still breathing, still living.

"Please tell me..." Tuck's breath filtered in through his nose. I could see his hamster wheel moving, the pieces being put together. "What in the actual fuck *are you* thinking?" That was just the fuck of it. I wasn't. Hell I still wasn't.

"No. I don't know what the fuck happened. I just know that I can't kill her. At least not yet." There was a piece of me that didn't want to think about her blood being spilled, one being that I had yet to know her, and two, she seemed too innocent for something like that to take place. I knew I was a bad man, a person with a less than stellar track record; but I couldn't hurt her.

The silence was unsettling between us as Tuck ran a hand over his bald head. It was a habit he had from back when he had hair. Now he just shaved it, making it easier for cleanup.

"Your option is to take her. Keep her in your suite and not allow the other men to know." Tuck sounded as shocked as I looked at the idea of keeping her a secret. Yet, it was the one and only idea that currently made any sense, but it was also the most dangerous.

"Fuck!" I cursed. I knew there was no going back now. I had already made the decision to keep her alive. Now I had to follow through with it. Turning the engine over, I threw the vehicle in drive, and headed towards the house. How could I be nervous over something as small as the woman in the back of my SUV?

"She's going to get you killed," Tuck reminded me.

"As if I already didn't know that, but so is anything and everything else I do!" I exclaimed, turning onto one of the side streets. Tonight wasn't about killing, it was about getting pussy. But somehow I was getting far more than I bargained for.

"You know she has to die no matter what. Putting it off won't make it any easier or worse…" Tuck tried to sound sincere, but I realized in his words just how much of a pussy I had to look like.

"I'm aware she has to die. She watched us murder someone, that's besides the point. I'm going to get what I want from her, take it if I have to. Then and only then will I watch her bleed out." The words rolling off my tongue disgusted me, but so did the fact that it bothered me to think of killing her. Tuck must've seen the anger in my eyes because he seemed to pull away a bit.

"I'm just trying to remind you man. I don't want you becoming attached if you know what I mean." He winked as if he was trying to attempt a joke, but I found it completely humorless. I knew what he meant, so did the other men we lived with and worked with. One had become attached to another female not that long ago, almost going as far as wanting to quit the syndicate, and go out and live a normal life. We couldn't allow that to happen, so we did away with her.

Turns out it made him into an even more ruthless killer. I didn't ever want to find myself in a situation like that, so I would keep Ellie at a distance. It was the only thing I could do.

"Attached would mean I would have to like her, feel some type of emotion for her, and we both know that emotion isn't really my cup of tea." I turned off onto another side street. We were less than five blocks from the house, and my adrenaline was starting to pump, my heart pounding loudly in my ears.

"Emotions don't always have to be present at first. You should know that, fucker," Tuck shot back at me, but I was too caught up in my own head to respond. Instead, I headed down the alleyway behind our house, pushing the button on the garage door opener. The garage opened revealing that only one of the other three men was currently home. Relief coated my insides immediately.

Dangerous Ties by J.L. Beck

Why was I scared? Nervous even? These weren't emotions that I knew how to handle.

"Take her straight upstairs. I'll distract whomever is here," Tuck said, jumping from the car the second I put it in park. He didn't seem to care that he had to keep a secret, then again I had seen Tuck do a lot of shit and never said anything.

I nodded my head yes without a word said and opened the door. My steps were heavy as I headed to the back of the SUV, pushing the trunk button on the key fob. As the door swung open, my eyes landed on her lifeless body. Yes, her chest was moving at a slow rate, but everything else on her made her seem lifeless. Her makeup was smudged, her dress ripped from the struggle she had with me.

No emotions. Turn them off.

The man underneath all of this, deep in my skin, in my heart told me to let her go. If she could just run fast enough, escape fast enough then she would be free of any chance of death. She would get a chance to live.

But the other part of me, the man that I was right at this moment told me it could ruin everything. Not only my reputation, but it could very well be my life in place of hers.

"Coast is clear," Tuck yelled into the garage, startling me to the point where I almost drew my gun.

"Fuck! I need to get out of my head," I whispered to myself as I grabbed Ellie underneath her arms and hauled her up. Her feet dangled over my shoulder and down past my stomach.

She seemed to weigh nothing, her height was barely above five foot, and the most dangerous thing about her at the moment was the fact that she was still breathing. With a slam of the trunk, I headed towards the door into the house.

There's no going back now, Grayson.

I hurried up the stairs and into the foyer. The whole place was designed like a bachelor pad, my room being on the top floor. We had big screen TVs and a kitchen that was made for the wildest parties, but we also had our own spaces with our own private bathrooms, personal kitchens, and living spaces within rooms. Really there was no reason for us to venture outside of our floor if we didn't want to. We had everything we needed within a few feet.

Scurrying towards the elevator, I walked through the living room, my head twisting in every direction. I pushed the up key as many times as I possibly could. I knew if I got caught with her, my death and hers would be dooming.

When the elevator dinged, I stepped inside casually and headed towards the top floor. I held my breath until we made it there, Ellie's body still unmoving against my own.

"Fucking shit!" I about yelled as I stepped up to the door placing my key card inside to gain entry onto my floor. My head was a fucking mess. The second I stepped through the door, I placed Ellie on my bed and headed straight to the fucking shower. I couldn't think straight with another man's blood on my hands. That and Ellie was fucking with my head.

Emotions weren't my thing. Yet, they were coming to life right before me.

ELLIE

FOUR

My head felt heavy, my wrists ached, and my mouth seemed to be filled with cotton balls. I rolled to my side, my heavy eyes barely lifting open. I could feel softness beneath me, as if I was lying on a bed made of pillows. A faint smell entered my nostrils telling me I wasn't in my own bed. Parting my lips ever so slightly, I could feel material making it impossible for me to open my mouth all the way. Immediately the haziness that had consumed me lifted as panic arose.

The memory of how I had gotten here and what had happened hit me like a ton of bricks. There was no forgetting the things that Grayson did.

That my father had done.

Stay in the present, Ellie. I reminded myself.

I focused on what I could see and hear. The sound of water could be heard off in the distance. I was lying in a bedroom slash living room. A large TV was in front of me as well as a wall lined with books. A couch and chair sat to the right, and on the left side was a kitchen. My head felt heavy as I tried to gain my bearings, taking notice of what lay straight in front of me. A door. An exit. It had to be, the only other door was where the sound of water was coming from.

Try as I may to make my legs move, they wouldn't. They were like pools of jelly, and with my hands bound together there was no way for me to move them.

"Fucking Christ!!" I wanted to scream but instead I spoke the words softly. There was no point in drawing more attention to myself. I had met this man on a chance encounter. I knew it wasn't meant to be, I could feel it my bones.

His lips though, the way his heart beat under his shirt as he touched my skin was real. Grayson was the first real thing I had ever felt in my life, even if he was the type of man I had spent the better part of my life running from.

"Why did I bring you back here? I'm sure that is the first question you're asking yourself, and the second is why are you tied up?" Grayson's deep voice caused my body to vibrate to life. I turned sharply forcing myself to fall back onto the sheets. My eyes zoned in on him, his shirtless chest and his dark blue jeans that hung low on his hips. His hair was still wet causing pieces of it to stick up in all directions.

"I know why you brought me here!" I shouted, even though my words were muffled by the object restricting my mouth, defying everything inside of me screaming at me to stay quiet.

When I went out last night, my plan was to try and be someone new if only for one night. To find a man who was warm, caring, and could show me what love really was, even if it was only through physical actions.

Grayson smirked, it wasn't one that told me he thought I had said something funny, but more so one that had to do with being amused. He stood staring at me for a moment before crossing the room. Each step was fluent, it held authority, and it made my stomach erupt in fear. When he came to a standstill in front of me, he reached forward, causing me to flinch and untied the cloth from the back of my head, freeing my mouth from the intrusion.

"If I wanted to kill you, I would've done so already. You fail to see the difference between what I will do and what I can do." I bent my head looking up at him as he towered over me. He had to be at the very least six feet two, weighing close to two hundred pounds. The muscles in his neck grew tight, and I could see his jaw line tighten as he waited to hear what I would say.

Was there really anything for me to say? I was now a hostage, once again taken by the evil in the world. The only difference was: could I escape this life as I did the last.

"I know all about men like you. I should've followed my instincts the moment you offered me that drink!" I growled. I didn't want to look weak, I had done that my whole life.

I watched as a baffled look crossed his face and then he leaned into me, the smell of crisp water and soap invading my senses. "Your instincts were telling you to give in to me, your body knew what you wanted even if you were hesitant to whether I was deserving or not..." His fingertips dug into my jaw as he held me in place, his eyes staring intently into my own. Heat was coming off of him in waves, each one burning me as much as the last.

"There will be no *if* about when I take you, Ellie. It will simply be a when, because I didn't risk my life, my brothers lives, and my reputation for nothing." His words were a blood oath promise. One that scared the ever loving shit out me, but it also excited me in the most frightening ways.

Grayson was right. My body was betraying me. It didn't matter how scared he made me. It didn't matter how nervous I was to be alone with him now that I knew who he was and what he did. He already knew everything he needed to know about me. He knew my body lusted for him in ways it hadn't done for anyone else.

"Then you'll be taking me against my will..." I narrowed my eyes in anger. The outcome of all of this always ended the same. Death. If I had stayed with my father and his empire, then I would be dead. Being kept here like a pet would lead to the same outcome.

Grayson laughed, and I mean actually laughed. It was a deep, robust sound that caused my cheeks to grow pink. What had I said?

"Sweet Ellie..." He mocked me, his fingers tracing down the side of my face. I wanted to lean into his touch as if I had never felt another person's skin but forced myself not too. With my hands still bound behind my back, I had no other option but to dig my nails into his bed sheets. He leaned into my face, his eyes going straight towards my lips.

"I don't have to worry about you not wanting it. In fact, I'll get you to a place where you'll be begging for it. You agreed once, and I'm sure getting you to agree will be so much easier the second time around." The smugness of what he had said infuriated me. I wanted to gash his eyes out, bite his lip, and draw his blood.

"See…" His sweet breath casted over my lips. "I know what I'm doing."

"Is that so? Then what do you plan to do with me when you're done? Huh? You act like I don't know, like I have never experienced something like this." I blurted out without realizing I was giving him a little bit too much of an insight into who I really was. But I hated him for how weak he made me feel, and throwing in his face that this was nothing new somehow made me feel stronger.

Silence surrounded us, he seemed off track for a moment, as if I had hit him below the belt with my words.

"If you have been in this position before, then you know once you have fulfilled your duties that your time comes to an end." He didn't say the word death, but I knew what he meant. Death was the only meaning to an end when it came to men like my father and Grayson. I didn't know much about him, but from what I had gathered in those short minutes where he was mine, I saw a man who wanted to be loved, just as I did. A person looking for someone to love them and all the demons they housed behind closed doors.

"Kill me then. In fact, do it now. I would rather die than be forced to do something as degrading as fuck you. When I made the decision to go with you earlier, I didn't think you were a psychotic killer. Clearly I was wrong…" I had barely finished my sentence when I was yanked from the bed. My legs were like a pool of jelly causing the lower half of my body to dangle on the floor as Grayson held the rest of my body off the ground.

"You'll die when I see fit. Do you understand me?" he growled, angry that I had told him to kill me now. His anger only fueled mine, therefore I countered back.

"I'll die when I see fit." I could see the rage boiling as the hold on my arm grew tighter until I knew there would be a giant bruise.

"Defy me all you want. Push the boundary as much as you would like. Push *me* as hard as you would like, but don't be surprised when I push back." He smiled and released me, which in turn caused me to hit the floor with a hard thud. Then he walked away as if he didn't just ruin my life.

"I hate you," I whispered under my breath feeling tears behind my eyes, but I couldn't cry. I wouldn't allow that emotion to form.

"No you don't... but you will once I'm done with you." I heard his voice and without realizing it I looked up at him with tears in my eyes. And even though tears meant emotion, and emotions meant death, I no longer cared. At least not now.

It was far too late to not be seen as weak.

FIVE

I watched as a fresh tear fell from her dark blue eyes. In them I saw the kind of fear I tried to hide from for the better part of my life. See a man who's as bad as me, a man who's done as much wrong as me has had his own fair share of thing's he's afraid of in life.

Watching those tears she shed, not even knowing her story or what she had went through in life made me want to pick her up off the ground and cradle her. I wanted to tell her everything would be okay. That I had lied, and that I was going to do everything I could to save her from the evilness that was me, but even I knew that was lie.

You couldn't put someone like her in front of me and not expect me to consume her. To suck every ounce of good out of her. Once I was done I would spit her back out into the world, a darker, grittier version of herself.

"Save the tears for someone else," I growled, angrier at myself than I was at her. She looked defeated, like a dog that had begged for attention over and over again and in turn still remained neglected.

"You're heartless!!" She screamed at me, and I knew what she was saying was true. There was no truer statement than that one, and even though I didn't want to continue to break her down I had an image to uphold. I had to make sure she understood where her place was with me.

"You knew that the moment I killed that man right in front of you. Don't act like you didn't," I responded, now agitated and uncaring to her emotions. I needed a drink. A loud sob escaped her lips, and it took everything in me not to turn around and say something to make it better. Grabbing the whiskey off the dresser, I went back over to the bed and stepped right over her sobbing frame. Twisting the cap off the bottle, I allowed the aroma of the whiskey to take over my body.

This was the closest to warming my heart that I could get.

"I've been through this once in my life. Don't make me do it again." Her voice was a plea that resonated deep within me. Old wounds were being torn open. The very wounds that made me start this job.

"That's what life is all about…" I wasn't even sure what I was trying to say. Instead I poured some whiskey into my mouth, allowing the burning feeling to enter my throat, invading my senses. As soon as the liquid hit my belly, I felt the warmth cascade through me.

"What do you know about life, Grayson? You kill people for a living. You rip life from people. You know nothing… You think you're better than me? Than them? You're not better than anyone. If anything this only proves that you are less." My mind was a mess as I listened to her words rip me apart, yet the one thing that stuck out to me most was the fact that she had said *them*.

"Them?" I couldn't hide the irritation from my words. I felt like she was hiding something from me, which given that we didn't know one another meant it could be anything.

She wiped the tear streaks from the apple of her cheeks with her nose wrinkled up at me. "That's the thing about you and me. I'm running from my past, and you're living in it." Her words didn't make much, if not any sense to me, so I took another swig of whiskey and blocked the last comment from her mouth out of my head.

"I'm going to pretend that I didn't just hear you talk to me like you know one motherfucking thing about me!" My emotions were on edge, one moment I felt secure, and the next I felt like a grenade that had just been sent into the air.

It's her. My mind was caught in a place between Ellie and my sister. One I could still save, and the other I couldn't.

I didn't need my mind to tell me that. I knew it. I could feel the shift in the air that she had caused. I needed to end this and end it now.

"How rich, yet you can pretend to know me..." She seemed determined to have me kill her as if it was on top of her bucket list or something. I needed to find a way to shut her up, just so I could get my mind back to a place that I could handle. An unstable Grayson had the power to bring everyone in this city down.

Without hesitation, I placed the bottle on the ground. She was still bound which meant this would make the struggle all the more less.

I took a step towards her, with her hands and feet bound she was unable to move away from me. The fear in her eyes spiked, causing my insides to roll. Oh how I wanted to take that fear and crush it into a million little pieces.

"I need you to shut up. I need to get you out of my head, and because of that I'm sorry." I could see the confusion forming in her eyes as I dropped down to my knees, my hands going straight to her throat. I needed to cut off her air supply. I needed to shut her the fuck up, and the only way I knew how was to put her out. As soon as she realized what was taking place she gasped, a breathy *no* falling from her plump lips.

"It's better this way." I tightened my hold, her eyes filling with tears as I applied more pressure waiting for her eyes to drift closed. There was no struggle. It was simply as if she was giving herself over to me. As if she had finally come to the fact that there was no getting out of this alive. With her eyes closed, I released her; not wanting to kill her, but simply wanting to sedate her.

My heart was beating out of my chest as I shuffled away from her body. I didn't stop until my back hit the edge of my bed, and then I found the bottle of whiskey I had placed on the floor.

I drank it, gulp by gulp. Not caring that I would have a raging hangover tomorrow. No, nothing mattered. Not as much as finding that warmth and losing myself in it.

I might not know Ellie that well, but I knew something about both of us. We were yearning for the one thing neither of us could possibly have.

Dangerous Ties by J.L. Beck

Warmth.
Compassion.
Love.

SIX

"Ellie, sweet little Ellie." My breaths were heavy as I ran down the hall. Each step seemed to sound louder than the next. I could hear his footsteps matching the beat of my own. I had known him for a few years now, and the way he looked at me made me feel sick with each linger of his eyes across my flesh.

"Come out wherever you are…" His voice dripped with venom. I continued down the hall, coming to the stairs to the top floor of the mansion. I knew if I went up there, there would be no escaping his wrath. Instead, I opened the small crawl space door below the stairs. Fear coursed through my veins, my hands shaking as I placed the small door back in place. I situated myself in a small ball, looking through the tiny slits in the wood. I knew I needed to calm my breathing or I would be found, but my heart wouldn't stop beating out of my chest.

"Ellie, it's not very nice to hide from someone who just wants to offer you a hug…" A shiver ran down my spine. It was never a hug. It was never ever a hug. I wrapped my arms around my center tightly as his words roared through me.

"Where oh where could she be?" He sounded amused as he knocked on the wall right outside of where I was hiding. I could see the small wood piece in front of me vibrate. I was shaking, tears threatening to fall from my eyes.

"Is she here?" he screamed, beating against the wall across from me. I bit my lip, forcing myself not to scream out in fear. A scream would definitely get me discovered, and then I would have to face him.

"What about here?!" He slammed his entire body against the wall where I was hiding as if he knew I had been here all along. My nails *sank into my flesh as the wooden door keeping him out started to move, coming undone. I said a small prayer as his body ran into the side of the wall once again.*

He knew where I was, and there was nothing I could do to prove him differently.

"Ellie…" He whispered my name just as his body landed one last time, the wooden door falling away completely. It fell to the gold carpeted floor with a thud, the same thud my heart made as I looked deep into the eyes of the man that would someday be my husband.

"Never run from me, Ellie. NEVER!" He growled with anger, gripping me by the hair with an evil smile on his face.

A thin layer of sweat covered my body from head to toe. The nightmare had felt so real, even though I knew it wasn't. Blinking my eyes open I took a deep breath, pushing the memory of the dream from my mind.

Days seemed to have passed, but couldn't have been more than a day or two. I swallowed slowly, mouth dry, wondering when the last time I had a drink of water or eaten as my stomach began to grumble.

Feeling as if I could move my fingers again, I wiggled my arms seeing if they were finally free and was pleasantly surprised to find both arms and both feet had been freed.

The faint smell of whiskey surrounded me, and slowly the memory of Grayson squeezing the life from me came back. I clenched my fists, wanting to punch the piece of shit in the face, yet looking around the room and finding not one sign of him. I sat on the bed for a few more minutes, waiting to see if he would jump out from somewhere and attack me. My hands drifted up to my throat. There was no real pain, just a little tenderness as I pressed my hand against it. Looking around the room, I could see there was no presence of Grayson physically here right now.

Once the coast was clear, I managed to get up from the bed cautiously, praying that my legs would have enough strength in them to hold my weight. I needed to find some food, go to the bathroom, and see if I could escape through one of the windows before Grayson got back.

As soon as I got my legs to hold my weight I was running to the bathroom, not even stopping to take in any of the sights of where I was currently being held. The moment I finished I began looking for the kitchen, which to my surprise I discovered it was in the same place just on the other side. Everything seemed open, each space flowing into the other.

A tray of food sat upon a counter as if it were waiting for me. I blinked slowly, wondering if I should even eat it or not. Then my stomach decided to groan once more in hunger. *Fuck.* It felt like being with the man I ran away from all over again. *Drake.* The control, the emotional despair that only he could bring out in me.

"Just eat and get out," I muttered out loud to myself. If I knew anything, it was that I had a very limited amount of time to attempt to get out of here. Lifting the top of the tray, my mouth started to water. Placed on a white plate was a slab of meatloaf with potatoes and gravy. Who cooked this? Could someone have poisoned it? Would I risk it? The questions seemed to be stacking up, but I pushed them to the back of my head.

With just enough time I allowed myself to take in a few whiffs of the food before scarfing the entire plate down, each piece hitting the bottom of my belly like a rock being thrown into a lake.

"If you eat too fast you'll puke, and then I'll have to place another order for food." My head lifted, my ears perking up at his voice, my eyes scouring the room for his presence. There he sat in the dim lighting of the room, near his unlit fireplace. His form casting a shadow in the corner. He was sitting in one of the chairs I had failed to notice that was along one of the windows I hadn't gotten to look out of yet.

So much for a fast escape.

"I can't trust you." My words were honest as I stared at him. There was no clear set of emotions etched into his features. In fact, the only thing I could tell was that he looked tired, desperate, and maybe even a little lonely.

His jaw tilted up, the light making his face look like he harbored a darker side to him.

"Have I given you a reason to trust me?" His question was a trick, so I didn't dare answer, instead I narrowed my eyes in anger. "I didn't think so, nor will I ever. Doing so would give you a false sense of hope... That maybe, just maybe, I'll allow you to get out of this alive."

Everything here seemed darker and more dangerous. My hand drifted to my throat-a reminder of all that he could do, yet what he was saying didn't make sense when he had multiple chances to take my life from me.

"I see you thinking. I see you working something out in your head, a plan... maybe?" he murmured. His words weren't slurred, but from the bottle of whiskey in his hands I would say it wouldn't be long.

I shook my head, a few strands of my hair falling into my face. "I'm not working out a plan at all. Just trying to decide how I'm going to say fuck you when I leave this place... Because mark my words, I refuse to be a prisoner again." Grayson's eyes darkened in anger and understanding, and it was then I realized I had said far too much.

"Prisoner? Has someone held you against your will before?" His question was one that I refused to answer, and because of that I would practically be giving myself away. The only acceptable way to get out of answering him was to halfway answer him.

I bit my lip, the memories were all too real, at least in my mind. Except I could easily see my life here with Grayson turning into the same thing.

"Yes, and I refuse to talk about it. Don't ask me questions, and don't assume that I can't handle myself in a situation such as this one. I've been put through far worse." I tried to remain strong, or at least appear that way.In the eyes of a man like Grayson, if he saw the slightest bit of weakness he would pounce on it, causing every strong piece of who you were to crumble.

I'd already showed him how vulnerable I was. I wouldn't do it again.

The air around us seemed to change. There was a zing in the air, the kind you feel right before lightning strikes.

"I'll make you a deal then," Grayson spoke. I had been right, lightning was just about to strike.

"I don't make deals with the devil."

"You do today. You do as I tell you, you don't attempt any escapes, and give me what I want and need. And at the end of all of this, I will let you go." My heart was beating heavy in my ears. Had he just given me a way out? No one had ever given me a way out before...

"How? I mean... I don't believe you." I stumbled over my words, shocked that he had offered something that couldn't be true.

It's a sense of false hope, Ellie. Don't believe a wolf in sheep's clothing.

Grayson stood from his chair, everything in me told me run; after all he had silenced me twice already. Who was I to say he wouldn't do it again so soon? Yet my feet were stuck to the tile floor like boots in mud. My insides churned, and a strange sensation formed in my chest. Even if I was scared of Grayson and the things he could do, there was a still a small part of me that yearned to know him, to learn what made him tick. People weren't evil for no reason. It almost always stemmed from something in their past.

"It doesn't matter if you believe me, Ellie. What matters is my word, and I will do whatever I can to let you go. Even if it means my own death." With wide eyes, I stared at him. Was my mind playing tricks on me?

I didn't even know what to say... Instead, I stared aimlessly, feeling as if everything had been flipped upside down. I didn't know if I could believe him, not with all that had happened in the last twenty-four hours, but then again what other option did I have?

Not believing him didn't matter, it was his word against my own personal thoughts. The only thing I really knew was that my life now laid in his hands, because I was about to seal the deal with one simple word.

"Yes."

SEVEN

"You have got to be the dumbest fucker on the planet." Tucker snorted as I explained to him the details of Ellie and I's deal. I knew it wasn't the worst choice I had ever made in my life, but I needed to know more about her. Hearing that she had already once been in a bad situation told me that I couldn't be that man to her. I couldn't hurt her any more than I already had, even if it ruined me, or better yet got me killed.

"I don't know what else to do. I feel this piece of shit thing in my chest beating for the first time in years, you know since my sister…" I trailed off. I couldn't talk about it. There was no way for me to bring it up without wanting to destroy the person who took her life from me, and when you couldn't find said person that meant a lot of other people took the brunt of that person's abuse.

"Letting her go is way too fucking risky. There's no way it's going to happen. The second the men find out about her, she's dead. Then what, Gray?" He gloated. There was a fire in my veins that was begging to be released, but I held back knowing that it was my fault that she was here. Not his, not hers, just mine.

"I just don't know what else to do." I sounded so defeated, which wasn't like me at all. Hell, since Ellie came around, I had become the biggest pussy on the planet.

I headed towards the kitchen to get a glass of water. After last night I needed something that was going to hydrate me. I had to spend the entire night with Ellie, her body close to mine but not really as she pulled herself away every chance she got. She might have agreed to my terms, but it wasn't something she wanted to do. I could tell by the look in her deep blue eyes.

"Well, you might want to figure it out soon. The guys called not long ago. Said they were on their way back, that they had a meeting with the boss man and needed to discuss some things," Tuck retorted just as I came back into the living room. I had locked Ellie up in my bedroom, knowing that she wouldn't try anything dumb if she knew what was good for her.

"Maybe I should just tell them..." I went over the idea in my head. It sounded good out loud, but then again hearing her cry for life as they brought a gun to her head caused my chest to ache. I squeezed my hands together until my knuckles turned white.

"No. Just do what you can to keep her hidden," Tuck plainly stated, looking up at me from the TV. He was my longest standing friend amongst the others. He knew where any and all soft spots in my heart came from. He also was one of the only people who had my back when I went against the bosses back in the day. Back when I was certain he had something to do with *her* death. My sister.

I was already getting to a point where I wasn't sure if I could let Ellie go. From the moment I laid eyes on her in that club I wanted to possess her.

"I'll do what I can, but if it comes out I'm not going to be able to stop them." I knew it as much as Tuck did. If we were out voted then there was nothing I could do to keep her here with me, and the way it was looking I already was.

"Stop who?" My chest heaved, I could feel the sweat forming on my skin as my anxiety built. I had killed tons of men, but nothing had me more nervous than the chance of my brothers finding Ellie.

"Oh, the *Mets* are playing in the World Series. Somehow I doubt they're going to be able to hold against the *Kansas City Royals*," Tuck said, letting the lie fall from his lips easily as he covered my ass.

Cole's eyes drifted between the two of us. Then he dismissed us, walking away into the main kitchen. Cole was the playboy of the house. He took women as he pleased, his eyes and body did all the talking when he didn't have to.

Luke entered the house next, not too long after Cole. He was the one you had to watch out for. He could read anyone like a book, and with one wrong look he would be able to tell something was up. He was also the closest to our boss.

"You missed one of the best jobs I've ever been on, Gray." Luke's hand slapped me on the back hard.

"Oh yeah? Why was that?" I chimed back smoothly.

"Well first, boss had us at a strip club. Cole even brought a couple of the chicks with him," he said, casting a look over his shoulder. "Anyway, it was a bloody ass mess. We ended up taking five men out that owed money. Then we got to fuck the shit out of the strippers. I mean every hole, Gray. Ass, mouth, vagina. There wasn't a damn thing off limits." He chuckled.

Any day before finding Ellie, and I would've been laughing right along. Instead I was feeling disgusted simply from hearing about it.

I didn't know if what I was feeling towards Ellie was love or not, because I hadn't felt love for anyone besides my family, but I knew I felt a connection to her. I felt the need to protect her from all the evil in this world, even if I was the most evil thing within touching distance of her at the moment. I stayed silent, my eyes training to the game as I heard Dex enter through the garage. With a slam of the door, I knew we were going to be in for a long night.

"What's a matter, Dex?" Tuck asked before the question could escape my lips. Dex was the genius of us all. If anyone could get away with murder, it would be him. Not only could he execute the plan, but he would construct it as well.

"Meeting. Now." His words were clipped as he headed towards the business room, not even glancing at us. Luke and Cole followed behind him, their footfalls echoing down the stairwell.

"Let's go," I grunted at Tuck as I headed the same way. I knew better than to show any type of anger or exhaustion. To my brothers I didn't have a reason for anger, fear, or to be worn out. If I wasn't given what I wanted, then I could take it.

"Boss has a new job for us." Dex pulled out folders for every person in the room. I took a seat in my usual spot, just as Tucker walked in.

"Job? Nothing seems like it's a job with him nowadays," Tuck joked, but no one saw the humor in it.

"The woman in this folder is someone who needs to be found as soon as possible. Dead or alive." Dex was in full authority mode. I grabbed the folder, curious as to what kind of person we were up against. The folder felt light in my hands. That was until I opened it and my eyes skimmed over the black and white photo inside of it. The photo was that of a much younger Ellie. Maybe five years younger, but I could definitely still see her in the photo. In that moment, my heart sank into my stomach. I was an evil man, a killer even, but I knew better than to become one of those people. The ones that double-crossed the boss.

"Who is she?" I blurted out, not wanting to try and sound overly interested. After all, we were both as good as dead if they found out I was hiding her upstairs.

"The boss' daughter." Dex's eyes met mine right as he tossed his folder down onto the table in frustration.

"I've been looking for her on my own for a month now with no leads. Apparently, she walked out on her fiancé and was never seen again. Her father has given all hope on her listening and learning to live with the life he had given her, and now he doesn't care if she is brought in alive or not." Dex didn't seem to care that the reasoning behind our boss' motives to kill his own daughter were nonexistent. Nothing in anything that Dex had said made sense to me. There was no true meaning to kill Ellie. Simply because her father felt she had disobeyed him? She was an adult.

Like I had said before, when I killed people I did so with a cause or attempted to do so. I wasn't just working for boss any more, I was on the hunt for my sister's killer. Knowing that Ellie was the boss' daughter told me there was way more to this story than Dex was letting on.

Dangerous Ties by J.L. Beck

"Any idea where she is?" Tucker questioned next. The way is his eyes bleed into mine told me he was just as concerned with the news as I was.

"Word on the street is that she lives in this area." A sigh from Dex filled the room. My eyes lifted to Luke's. He was watching me, or maybe he wasn't and I was just one paranoid bastard.

"Should be easy to find her then." Cole smirked. He was the lover boy, and had I not got Ellie first, Cole would've been the next person to lure her in with the flash of his pretty white teeth. He was the true wolf in sheep's clothing in our group.

Alarm bells were going off in my head, ringing non-stop. I knew, now more than ever that I had to do something with her.

Looking down I noticed that I was white knuckling the shit out of the folder. *Deep breathes, Grayson. Deep fucking breaths.*

I could feel eyes on me, and just as I looked up to see who it was that had spotted my mixed emotions, Dex's phone rang. His ringtone filled the room with an annoying ding. We all watched as he looked at the caller id before finally answering.

"This is Dex." He kept his voice void of all emotion, but I could see the annoyance in his eyes. Sometimes I thought Dex and I could be closer if he wasn't so far up the boss' ass.

"8ᵗʰ street?" Dex asked, his eyes growing dark. He grabbed a pen from the table and started writing on the back of his folder of information. Whoever was on the other end of that phone was giving him directions.

"We'll deliver, we always do." Dex smiled, hanging up the phone.

"Hot fucking damn, more bloodshed?" Cole, shoved from the table with way more enthusiasm than he should've for someone who just got to kill, but I guess that was the thing about all of us. We thrived off of very different things, Cole's thing was blood.

"Hit the Tahoe boys, we've got a kill to make." Tremors worked their way through my body slowly as I stood, placing the folder on the table. Ellie was going to be as good as dead, and so was I.

Neither of us would be able to walk away from this now.

ELLIE

EIGHT

Hours seemed to have passed since I signed my own death certificate. When I awoke the smell of blood and danger was in the air. I blinked my eyes open trying to figure out why darkness was all I could see. Fabric could be felt across my eyelids and against my wrists, restraining me from seeing or moving. And as panic formed in my chest, I felt the soft caress of a hand down my chest.

"I should've resisted you. I should've left you in that alley." Grayson's voice was like liquid smoke. It filled my lungs, breathing some type of life back into me.

"Why am I restrained?" My words hung in the air for a long moment as I felt the softness of the fabric rub against my flesh. The silence caused a shudder to run down my spine as each second in between him responding ticked away.

"I... I... I told you I would do whatever you wanted." I stumbled over my words trying to figure out what the hell was going on. His darkness surrounded me, waking parts of my body that hadn't been awakened in years.

"We had an agreement, and now you must pay..." I knew what he meant, he wanted my body and no matter how much I told myself I wouldn't feel anything from his touch, I knew that it was all a lie. That my body craved his touch more than it ever had anyone, so I gave in easily.

"Take what you want," I told him, my voice not my own.

Dangerous Ties by J.L. Beck

His footsteps echoed off the wood floor, and I couldn't tell if he was walking towards me or away. All I knew was that I didn't want him to leave yet.

"Oh sweet, Ellie." He laughed gruffly. "I won't be taking what I want. That's not how I work." I blinked behind the blindfold, unsure of how I felt about what he had just said.

"Every second that I possess your body, will be a second that you enjoy. I won't take what I want, but I will give you what you need, what you desire..." Hot breath hit my ear, and I shuddered. My core grew wet with desires for a ruthless man, a man that had wrapped his hand around my throat and sent me into an unconscious state more than once.

My breath hitched in my chest as I felt his hand glide over my throat and down, stopping between my breasts. Unable to conceal what he was doing to my body, my heart pounded in my chest.

"I... can't..." The words wouldn't come out. I just knew that I couldn't let anything happen between us, anything that would cause me to self-destruct.

"Shhh..." Grayson's lips settled onto my own, the harsh, firmness of them taking me back to that night in the alley where he turned my world upside down. "You can, and you will," he whispered softly, and then it was as if the man I had previously met vanished. It was as if a mask had been lifted and thrown to the floor.

I could do nothing to stop him from ravishing me; from destroying me from the inside out. His teeth nipped at my bottom lip, forcing me to open up to him. His hands roamed my body roughly, as if he was searching for a hidden treasure.

"I want to touch you," I whispered. I didn't even recognize my own voice. Nothing in that moment mattered more than feeling his body against mine. If I was going to die, then this would be the perfect way to go out.

Leaving one hand against my hip, he took his other one and untied my hands from the bed railing. Without hesitation I gripped his hair pulling him closer to me.

Closer. I need him closer. I told myself.

"It's nothing more than an agreement." Grayson's words were soft, as he gripped my hips in his hands. I couldn't see the look on his face because of the blindfold but I knew if I could, that he would look different, less dark, less cold. I knew there was no going back after this.

Taking a deep breath, I lurched forward putting every single emotion I could into that one single kiss. My fingers combed through his hair, and my lips ground against his as he deepened the kiss, pushing off that last rock we were sitting precariously upon.

Grayson's hands weaved underneath me, and in a flash I was sitting on his very naked lap. A gasp wanted to escape me, but he refused to let it, taking the moment to ravish me once again.

"Your mind, your body, and your soul are mine for one singular night." His words slipped out as he cascaded kisses down my neck and onto my chest. I took the chance to pull the blindfold off and get one last look at him, and as I did I was shown just how much he was exposing himself.

Grayson gave me a sexy smile before pulling my tank top off. My cheeks grew red as I realized I hadn't put a bra on.

"So full and firm," he whispered, pulling my nipple into his mouth as his other hand gripped my breast. I tried not to blush knowing that I had done far worse things than what he was currently doing to me. Pleasure filled my veins, and my blood soared as my emotions started to spiral out of control.

Never had a man brought me to my knees so easily.

Grayson was my weakness and would ultimately be my death. I knew it, and I was sure that he knew it by now as well.

With a loud pop he released my nipple from his mouth and with it went every ounce of pleasure. Regret started to form deep inside of me, but before I could even say a single word Grayson was stripping me completely bare. My sleep pants, along with my panties were thrown to the grown. I was exposed to this man, this man that I wanted to care for, but at the same time didn't know if I could trust.

"When you were with him did he make you come, Ellie?" A shiver ran down my spine for more than one reason. How did he know about him, and why did he care if he gave me pleasure or not? I held still, my heartbeat rising with every passing second as he watched me closely. His eyes roamed my body, promising me things that I knew could never be true.

No," I said without further thought. I didn't want to lie to Grayson. The only person whom brought pleasure to me was myself. His lips lifted in a dark smile, his hand lifting to trace the contours of my face. He watched me, looking for some type of emotion in my features, whatever it was he was looking for though, he wasn't getting. Not from me.

"Well, I'm going to bring you to the brink of exhaustion tonight. I'll push you to the boundary between pleasure and pain, and then…" His face came down to my ear. His teeth nipped at my skin, and goosebumps swarmed me. He was like a hot knife through butter. Smooth. And he melted me straight to the core. "I'll do it all over again," he finished.

My body shook with his words, the thought of what he could do to me taking over in my mind. Seconds passed where we stared at one another and then he was on me, possessing me in a way he hadn't before. His hands were in my hair and down my back.

I could finally feel every inch of him. His cock was pressed firmly against my core, causing a shiver to travel down my spine

"Don't be shy. He's ready for you." Grayson's voice was velvet. I swallowed the lump in my throat and gripped him firmly in my hand. He was large, his head swollen with just a small amount of pre-cum on it. I wanted to lick it away and see if he would mewl in the darkness for more.

At the thought, my pussy clenched with a need like never before. Grayson must've saw it in my eyes, because in a moment I was pushed to my back, my legs spread, while his hot breath fanned against my entrance.

"I want you to know that your pussy is beautiful." Grayson's lips fell against my inner thigh, and a sigh almost escaped me. Never had my ex fiancé, gone down on me. He considered it disgusting. Now here I was about to experience it for the first time with a man I barely knew.

My stomach flip-flopped as Grayson's thick digit entered me. This would be the first time since…

"When I tell you to take my cock, you take it." Spit clung to my face as he pressed me further down onto his cock. My throat burned and

my eyes began to water, but I knew if I didn't do this, something worse could happen.

"Ellie…" Grayson said my name with more concern than needed, and as soon as my eyes popped open I knew why. I had a flashback, to events from the past with a man not even worth mentioning.

"I want you," I begged, knowing he would stop if I told him where I just went. That I had climbed back into my own mind, clinging to the darkness of my past.

He watched me with caution before slowly entering me with his finger again. My pussy clenched around him without thought, and my nails dug into his back. I could feel the tingly sensation building deep inside of me as he worked himself in and out, adding another finger slowly.

"As you come I want you to think of me, and the next time you play with yourself I want you to picture riding my face." My senses were starting to shut down, but I still caught what he said as he removed his fingers and replaced them with his tongue.

"Whattt… Ahhhh…" I couldn't even get the why out to his question because every nerve on my body was on edge. My toes curled as his tongue swirled around my clit. One second he was entering me with it and the next he was licking and sucking in a manner that reminded me of eating ice cream. My legs shook as a wave of pleasure hit me.

Everything felt hotter as my body went into overdrive. His hands gripped my hips firmly holding me in place as he licked every drop that dripped from me. I gripped the sheets with all my might, praying he would stop, praying he'd never stop at the same time.

"Say my name, Ellie. Purr it. Scream it. Because I won't stop until you can't grip these bed sheets any longer." My head shot up as a scream escaped me. I was coming, and it was nothing like I had ever been able to do for myself. Grayson's fingers dug deeper into my ass, keeping my pussy in line with his face as he lapped at me, skimming between my folds with his nose and tongue.

Dangerous Ties by J.L. Beck

By the time he was finished, my legs were jelly and I was spent. Never in my life had I come this hard before, but this man, this devilishly, evil man named Grayson had proven me wrong.

"I don't think I can take much more," I moaned into the pillow against my face. I was sweaty and thoroughly worked over, and my lady bits had never been so on fire. Grayson had shown me something no one ever had, and I would cherish that no matter what.

"Oh, there is much, much, much more where that came from." He laughed, gripping his cock in his hand as he nudged me over onto my belly. I turned my face out, so I could look at him over my shoulder, and the sight I caught was one I will never forget.

There was a look of longing in his soft grey-blue eyes. He traced a line down my curved spine, and I fell into his touch so easily, wanting more of it as soon as his finger left me.

Then just like clouds after a storm the look was gone. Our eyes met over my shoulder as I watched him grab a condom and slide it on. My lips watered, and my stomach filled with butterflies as I felt him press against my entrance.

"Do you want it hard?" His hand lifted into my dark brown hair, pulling my head back causing my scalp to burn. "Or soft?" I could feel his lips at the base of my neck. I didn't know what I wanted. I just knew I wanted him, however I could have him.

"I don't care how it happens, I just want you." With a deep growl of approval, or maybe it was something else, he entered me hard. I was pushed forward, my face resting firmly on the pillow with my ass in the air as he pounded into me. Each glide of his cock forced his balls to smack against my clit.

"Ahhh..." I couldn't keep the moan of pleasure in any longer. My fingers gripped the pillow beneath me tightly, and as I felt the distinct build of an orgasm forming I wondered if it could get much better than this.

"Do you want to come? I can feel that sweet pussy clenching like a vice every time I slide in. Just like this..." He slid in as far as he could go, smacking my g-spot right in the face with his dick.

"Please..." I pleaded with him. The pleasure was almost pain as it continued to build. My toes curled, and my bones felt as if they were melting, but he refused to let up. Instead he pulled out, only to slide in as slow as he could, causing every single hair on my body to stand on end.

"Beg for it," he grunted. Grayson's voice was deeper and darker than usual telling me he too was close to the edge.

"I want to come. Let me come. Please…" I gasped as he grinded himself against me. My body tightened and I could feel the moment he allowed me to come, because it was the same moment he also allowed himself, too.

With three more hard slams into me, we were both panting one another's names as we rode out our orgasms.

I had never felt so connected, yet disconnected to someone…

NINE

When I awoke the next morning, I wasn't sure if what had happened between Ellie and I was a mistake or godsend. Knowing she had craved me with the same desires all along caused the coldness in my chest to seep away, but it also made things a lot more complicated.

I could tell sex was far more to her than it ever was to me from the second I slid into her. The way her eyes rolled lightly as I slammed in again and again. Most women couldn't handle a man in control, and I didn't think she could either, but she took everything I gave her without plea.

Staring silently into the morning light that casted upon us, I knew that today would be the end of anything that had started. I had caused this mess, and now I had complicated it further. Deep down somewhere inside the pitiful darkness of me, there was a man that longed for someone like her.

My sister would've loved her.

I couldn't go there. I couldn't think about her and not want answers to my questions. Therefore, I shoved her to the back of my mind once more.

Why dwell on the past when you can't go back to alter the future? Instead I forced my attention to Ellie and her still sleeping form next to me. It wasn't a surprise to me that she was still sleeping. We had sex three more times last night, and I knew more than anyone that she was going to be a slow riser from that alone this morning.

My eyes glided over her dark hair and alabaster white skin. She was so fragile, like a flower in a field that had the potential to grow into something big given the right living conditions. I wanted her to have that potential.

For a few moments I stared, my eyes going straight to her parted lips. They were a dusty pink color and slightly bruised from my kisses last night, yet as I kept my eyes on them I could feel it in my chest that I wanted nothing more than to see a smile form on her lips every day that I was alive.

Warmth seeped into my bones, and just as I was going to lean over and place a soft kiss on her shoulder my phone buzzed on the nightstand. Immediately, anxiety took place of any happy feelings I had previously had.

Exhaling a breath of air, I rolled over and grabbed my phone. I had a couple texts from the guys, but nothing stood out to me quite like the one from Tuck.

6:53 AM Tuck: Something's up.

6:58 AM Tuck: I'll try to cover as long as I can to buy you some time.

7:00 AM Tuck: They know.

I gripped my phone in my hand, another breath leaving me. It was starting to feel the same way it had when I lost *her*. The walls were closing in around me. Hands were clamping around my neck, and oxygen was no longer filtering into my lungs. I couldn't go on with this anymore.

"Grayson…" Ellie's voice blanketed me in warmth, pulling me from the murky memories and thoughts of my own mind, and God how I wanted to keep her for myself. It was as if she was an angel sent down from the heavens to bring me back to the good side. To remind me of all that is great in life.

"Grayson, are you alright?" The way she said my name reminded me of last night, and the many nights that I could have her as my own if I just could…

This is what you get, Grayson. The one thing you want more than life in your grasp, only to know that it has to be taken away.

I shook my head. I knew I had to do something. I had to uncover her secrets, and I needed to do so without exposing too much of myself.

Dangerous Ties by J.L. Beck

"What we shared last night was amazing..." I started out, not wanting to scare her away. However, I needed her to know that what had happened wouldn't happen again. I had come to that conclusion after all of the unsaid feelings I got this morning.

"Usually the woman says that, or something like... this can't happen again, it was a mistake." She smiled and as her lips lifted, I felt everything inside of me that was dark evaporate.

"Well that's not the case here. It can't happen again for numerous reasons." I paused, watching the light leave her eyes. My words hurt her. I understood it though, because it hurt me, too.

"Go on..." She concurred.

"We need to discuss some things regarding you and your past." I kept my features neutral, watching her eyes as panic settled deep within them. A storm was brewing under the surface. I was just curious when the first lightning bolt would strike. Placing my phone back on the nightstand, I stood from the bed. I couldn't sit next to her knowing that I was about to rip apart everything good that we had just shared.

"My past has not a damn thing to do with you." Her chest rose and fell as anger formed on her face.

I tried not to laugh, but a non-amused chuckle left my throat. Miss Ellie had no idea how wrong she was about that.

"I know your past is littered with a darkness similar to my own, and that you're barely hiding it underneath all the shit you use to tell yourself that it's still not there, not haunting you." Surprise showed on her features, which in turn, turned to rage.

"You know nothing about me, Grayson. Nothing but what I want you to know, so before you start comparing me to you, realize that you don't have a damn clue what my past consists of." Her small hands were balled up into fists, and her cheeks were glowing red. She had pissed off written all over her face, yet again I had to tell her just how fucking wrong she really was.

"Ellie, you can lie to everyone else, but I already told you who I was and what I was capable of. You believing me had not a damn thing to do with me." One of my hands ran through my hair vigorously because I knew what I was about to say was going to be the atomic bomb on her pissed off face.

"I don't give a fuck what you do, or who you kill! You act like you're the first criminal I have ever been with? Spare me the fucking details, Grayson…" She growled and shoved from the bed, obviously not able to sit any longer either.

"I need to know everything, Ellie." I tried not to sound desperate, but she didn't know all I truly wanted to do was save her. Get her out of here, but yet keep her close to me at the same time.

Her lip curled up in a snarl. "You don't need to know shit."

"I do, because your dad is looking for you, and he hired my team to find you." The bomb had been dropped right in her lap. She took a staggered step back as if I had physically slapped her. One hand went to her mouth covering up whatever cry was going to leave her lips, while her eyes began to water with fresh tears that refused to fall.

Never had I wanted to comfort someone more in my entire life. I knew the moment that I looked at her and watched the defeat take over her body that her father had done her wrong in more than one horrible way. Hell, I knew who her father was and the fact that I knew nothing of him having a daughter told me he didn't really give a fuck about her from the start.

"Oh God… this can't be happening…" Her dark blue eyes were frantic, her voice high pitched in fear. She knew far more than she was letting on, that much was true right now.

"It is… which is why I need you to be extremely honest with me. I need to know everything…" I tried to remain cool about everything, but I couldn't help my feelings based off of her reaction. I was angry, fuming, and sad all at the same time, simply because I knew there was not a fucking thing we could do to get ourselves out of this situation.

"I need to leave. I need to run. Go into hiding." Her voice and eyes seemed distant, as if she was closing in on herself.

"No. No…" I crossed the room in a breath, my hands reaching out to grab her and hold her in place.

"Yes, Grayson!" Her eyes were vacant of the Ellie I had seen previously. In them lingered so much sadness and fear that I couldn't comprehend what he had even done to her. "My father is a horrible, disgusting man, and if he finds me I'm dead. Hell,

I'm dead now if he's hired you to find me." She seemed to pull from my touch, as if my hands burned her skin.

"Ellie, I told you before I wanted to let you go. That the plan all along had been to let you leave..." I was about to find myself in hotter water.

"Let me leave? The plan was to let me leave even when you knew that my father wanted my head on a stake?" She laughed, but it wasn't humorous; instead it was full of anger and aggression.

"I just found out about the bounty on your head, Ellie. I didn't know who your father was until I received the folder with your name on it. The guys that live here with me don't know that I have you here, they don't know that you're the one person we're searching for..." I sounded defeated and believe me when I say I was, but I wanted to try and keep her calm.

She scowled. "So now what are you going to do? Sell me out to them? I'm as good as dead either way. I can't remain hidden here forever, I would rather die than be confined to a living-quarters ever again."

Bile rose in my throat. That was just the thing, how was I supposed to let her go, or even get her out of this place without them finding out. Better yet, once they did find her, because they always did, what would happen to the two of us? Would I have to be the one to put a bullet in her head?

I wasn't sure Ellie knew just how close to death she was. Or maybe it was me that didn't want to admit how big of a killer I was going to have to be?

TEN

Coldness settled deep into my bones, exposing the flesh wounds of my past. That was the thing about time, it was like a temporary band-aide. It covered up the past, but eventually something would come along and rip the wound back open, exposing all the darkness and sadness to you again.

I could tell from the way Grayson watched me that he understood, at the very least part of how I felt.

"Just sell me out to them, Grayson. Make it easier on yourself. Tell them that you found me first..." I snarled, angry mainly at myself for getting into this situation. I knew I shouldn't have ever followed him out of that bar, but I also knew that I craved something about him.

Grayson rolled his eyes angrily, gripping me by the shoulders. I was barely keeping the sheet up between the two of us, the sheet that shielded my naked body from his clothed one.

"Are you deaf? I'm not outing you, Ellie. I can't. As much as I want to keep you here, I know I can't because it's not safe." His voice took on a tone I hadn't heard before, one of complete defeat.

"I hear what you're saying, I'm just not hearing the logic behind it. I'm wanted by a notorious king. There is a bounty on my head, and you were hired by my father to kill me. What about any of that says safe?" I could feel the sweat forming on my hands as my past drug me under.

"Ellie!!" My father's thunderous voice echoed in my ears. I knew that tone, it was one that made me cower in fear.

Dangerous Ties by J.L. Beck

"Yes, father," I said as sweetly as I could, without getting my tongue caught in knots. I had never been able to handle his rage the right way, sometimes all was okay, and other times I was beaten for giving him the wrong tone.

"You're almost of age now." He smiled, and it caused my stomach to churn. I knew what he was going to bring up. It had been something he had been in negotiations with since my birth. I was now sixteen, on the verge of having an arranged marriage. My father insisted that it was for the greater good of the family, but I knew better having known who would be my husband all along.

"Yes, father," I agreed, knowing that my protest would go unheard, or they would be heard and would result in a beating. One that I would hope would be my death.

"I won't let them kill you, Ellie. I'm a bad man myself, and I've done some really horrible shit, but I can see it in your eyes… I know your past without words even being said, and if I ever needed to do the right thing it would need to be right now." Grayson's voice had filtered into my ears, surpassing the sound of my father's belt against my back.

"This is the end, Grayson, when your gang finds out that I've been here, right under their noses it's not going end with a happily ever after." The truth was, I would rather Grayson kill me now than wait a minute longer for the rest of his men to find out about me and come up here and kill me themselves.

"Listen to me… I'll…" I could hear the loss for words in his voice. He didn't even know what he was going to do.

"Have you worked for my father all along?" I blurted out, my eyes finally focusing in on him. His mouth opened to answer me but then closed. That was the only answer I needed. Knowing that Grayson had been a part of that evil man's plans this whole time made my insides burn. It made me feel dirty for even breathing the same air as him. If only Grayson knew of all the bad he had done to me.

"I didn't know he was your father. I swear to God." He pleaded with me as if we had a relationship, and I could walk out that door and leave him here to his lonesome.

"Yet, you worked for him. You knew all the horrible things he's done, I mean he's had you do them." I was a basket case. Concerned about things that I could no longer change.

"I need to know everything. I need you to tell me about your past, why your father is after you, and why he doesn't care if you're found dead or alive?" I listened to his words, but felt none of them truly hitting me. I was freezing over. Dropping the sheet to the ground, I gathered up my clothes and put them on ignoring him the best that I could.

Silence was all I gave him, all he really deserved from me.

"I know you're hurting, but your father isn't the only one who hurt you. He hurt me too, years ago when I wanted to leave, to get out and try and do better for myself." That statement stopped me. It forced a breath from my chest and caused me to turn around and face him.

"My sister was everything to me, the last living family member I had. Everyone else was taken out or passed away of old age. My sister was all I had left. She was only a little younger than me, she had a life full of dreams. Then one day she was gone. Dead to the world. I'm pretty sure your father had something to do with it, but there is no proof." The look of anger that showed in his eyes told me just how much hate he had towards him.

"I'm..." I didn't want to be like everyone else and say I'm sorry, because being sorry meant you felt some type of connection to that emotion. Right now I had no connection to what Grayson was going through. I understood his anger, but I didn't know death like he did.

"I don't need you to be sorry. I just want you to understand. To be able to open up to me because I can't save you..." He paused a moment, looking me straight in the eyes. "I can't get you out of this without knowing what I'm up against." My body shook with tears that refused to escape my eyelids.

"I don't think revisiting the past is going to change the future, Grayson?" I didn't mean to sound so hateful, but I had lived in the past my entire life. I knew better than to go down that road again.

"I don't want to revisit the past to change the future, Ellie. I want to revisit the past to make sure we don't make the same mistakes twice." Calmness settled over me as I realized what he was saying. I wanted to believe all that he said would come from reliving the past, but I knew mistakes weren't made twice. They were simply never a mistake to begin with.

"The past should stay in the past," I whispered and then my heart sank as I dove deep into my memory to tell him the story of how I became the broken shell I call myself.

ELEVEN

Two things are always true about life: You're born, and then you die. What you did, or do in that time between is up to you. I tried to remember a time in my life when I wasn't afraid, but the truth was I had always been afraid. Always running, always lingering in the shadows, too afraid of my own reflection.

I had lived under my father's thumb for so long I didn't know what it was like to breathe without being told that I could do so. My body was beaten and used by others at their own will all because of him. He was my father... he was supposed to save me, protect me from the evil in the world.

Instead, he didn't. He found a man darker than him, to rule my life far worse than he had. Drake. He was dark and brooding, his smile was one I loved in the beginning, but that was before I knew what the plan was. Before everything changed. My father, who in secret I called Daniel, his first name, had made the arrangement with the Dior family.

"I'm tired of telling you this, Ellie. I'm tired of reminding you of what your birth was even for!" Daniel snarled at me, his eyes black as coal. I was tired of reminding him that I wasn't some whore that could be passed off from man to man.

His hand lifted, the back of it hitting me along the cheek. I knew nothing of love or compassion. It wasn't the first time a hit had been given. It was his only way of controlling. Abuse. Breaking. If he could make you feel weak then he had all the control. My head fell to the side, my hair shielding my face from his view.

"I don't care what Drake has done to you. You will marry him and seal the fate between our two families. Otherwise, I will kill you myself."

Dangerous Ties by J.L. Beck

His words stuck against my skin as if they had been glued there. Daniel was evil, but he had never threatened me with death. And from the look in his eyes, I knew better than to question him.

I nodded my head in understanding for the last time, pushing the tears away. I couldn't cry again, not for any of them. Instead, I would do whatever I could to get away from it. It didn't matter to me if I was caught or not, death would occur no matter what happened. My only option was to run. Hide and never be seen again.

Taking what little money I had, one of my father's men drove me to a diner on the south side of New York. From there I took the subway and decided that I was no longer going to be me. I dyed my hair, got contacts, and picked up a low profile job working during the day at a restaurant.

That was who he forced me to become, I thought to myself as the retelling of my fated life came to an end. By the time I was done speaking tears had started to fall. In the end you dealt with the cards you were dealt in life. I couldn't change the hand, but I could draw a new card to better my deck.

"I…" Grayson's eyes were so soft and tender. He looked at me like I never wanted him too: like a victim. I was not what happened to me, but what I chose to become.

"Stop!" I began. "I don't want your pity, Grayson." Tears still welled behind my eyes, but I brushed them away. I didn't need to spend any more time dwelling on this. Instead, I needed to find a way out. I had managed to hide once, I could do it again, and I would. Even if I had to find a way out of New York.

"I don't pity you. Not one fucking bit. If anything I'm pissed, pissed that your father refused to protect you. That he let people use you…" A growl escaped him. There was tension in his features as he spoke, his eyes casting down to the wooden floor.

I shrugged my shoulders. "I've long acknowledged what had happened and even sought out therapy. Nothing can change what happened all those years ago." I could feel the warmth of his hand on my shoulder. As much as I wanted to shrug it away and pretend like it didn't melt me a little, I couldn't. Having let him know my story made him the closest person to me.

"I can't change your past, but I will help change the future. I promise to come up with a way to get you out of this. I can't let you go back to your father. Not now, not ever again." There was so much strength in his words, it was as if he truly believed them.

"I won't count on it, but since you're the only person to ever know about what happened, I will give you the benefit of the doubt." I smiled softly. A weight had been lifted from my shoulders. No longer did I feel weighed down by past events. At least if I died tomorrow I would have one person that knew my secret. That understood why I ran.

"I have a friend, a man named Tuck. He lives here with me and the others, but he's always had my back." Grayson seemed unsure about telling me, but I'm sure he realized we were way past keeping secrets anymore. I had already been here for days. That, and I remember meeting a man named Tuck the night they brought me here.

Silence passed between us, I didn't know where to go from here. Now it was about life and death, survival and endurance, because I knew if I didn't make it out of here there was a chance Grayson wouldn't either. Not after his team found out what he did.

"It's going to be okay. I know your past tells you to run, but you've been running long enough." His voice was comforting, but his words weren't. He didn't understand. Running was your only choice when it came to death. Die or run from the things chasing you. I got by with small pieces of living, even while on the run.

"Grayson..." I sighed into the air, pushing a few pieces of hair behind my ear. I wanted him to understand because he was the closest person to me at the moment, but I knew he was naïve to think I was getting out of this alive.

"Don't act like we can't try. I brought you here without knowledge of your past or who you were. It was completely bad luck that you came up on the kill list, but I won't tell you again. I will do whatever it fucking takes to make this right." He growled, ignoring me and anything I had said about the matter.

"Do what you must, Grayson, but just know I'll be preparing for my own funeral." It wasn't a lie. My funeral would be the next big thing to take place in my life. I knew my father and all that he was about. There was no negotiating. Grayson knew that as well.

That's why his faith in getting us out of this situation shocked me.

He believed in something he shouldn't believe in, or rather someone.

Me.

TWELVE

My hands were sweating as I walked down the hall.

Each level of the building had its own floor for each of us. Tuck was right below me, which made it easier to hide Ellie and her footsteps as she walked around on the top floor. I wiped the sweat away on my pants before making a fist to knock on the door. As far as I knew I looked like a man who was more than hiding a secret. More so like a dead body.

My knock echoed through the hall as I waited for Tuck to answer the door. Seconds passed, and the sweat seemed to pool. My stomach was in knots, when I had I ever been this nervous before?

Your first kill back in the day, I thought to myself.

"Grayson, what the fuck?" Tuck's deep voice rang in my ears as he opened the door. I shoved in, pushing past him and slamming it behind me.

"You said they knew..." I couldn't really hide the panic from my own voice. I ran a hand down my face and through my beard.

Tuck blinked, "Well they don't know it's her. They know you had someone with you last night. A woman. They saw her on the cameras when you brung her into the building."

Fuck! That was the last thing I needed, them snooping, and if anyone was snooping it was one of two people. Cole or Dex.

"Even more of a reason to get her the fuck out of here. I made a mistake, Tuck. A huge fucking mistake." I cracked my knuckles, anger radiating from me. I hadn't made a bad choice since my sister's death. Her death wasn't my fault, but the fact that she died had made me feel as if I had failed her. It was my job as her brother to protect her from everything, and I knew that if I failed Ellie I wouldn't be able to forgive myself. In the beginning I said it wasn't personal, but now it was more than personal. It was revenge.

Tuck rolled his eyes, his lips lifting in a half smile as if to say I told you that a long fucking time ago. Which was true, he told me bringing her here would expose us. Women weren't allowed in the building, so now I needed an excuse and not just , but a good one.

"You're the only one I can go to about this. You were with me that night at the club." Fuck, coming out with this was harder than it seemed. Was I weak for developing feelings towards her, or weak because now that I knew what happened I wanted to kill the man behind all of this?

"First you're going to have to talk to Dex. From there it's going to be slow moving because if they got a good image of her, they'll know she's Ellie Goodwin off the bat, and then you're both better off dead," he answered. I clenched my fist harder. Anger was the only emotion I was feeling.

"I know what her father did to her, Tuck. I know everything; her past and her present. I have…" I trailed off, knowing I didn't want to finish the sentence.

"You're whipped, baited. You care, and now the whole fucking game is wacked," Tuck grumbled.

"Yeah, yeah, so now we need to get her out of here because she's a bleeding zebra underneath a pack of lions noses." The analogy fit well, because if Ellie was found she would be destroyed, as would I, because I know they wouldn't make just anyone take her out. They would make me do it. I didn't know if I could take a gun and place it against her temple, pull the trigger and ever be the same man again.

Tuck stared at me for a long moment before speaking, "What if you disguised her someway? We could tell the guys she's a paid prostitute or something?" He threw his hands in the air. "I honestly don't know. We could wait until they leave and simply sneak her out? You could deal with the questions later?"

I bit the inside of my cheek at the thought of the first idea, and then realized maybe Tuck was right. Maybe we were making this harder than it needed to be. Maybe the easiest way to get her out of here was the same as how we got her in here to begin with?

A light bulb went off in my head. If the plan didn't work we were all dead, but if it did then Ellie was free. Gone forever, but free.

"We need to find out when the next hit is taking place, let Dex know we're staying behind to deal with some shit, maybe investigate where Ellie could possibly be hiding, and then sneak her out into the parking garage?" Tuck looked at me sideways.

"Alright, and if we're caught?" His eyebrow raised in a challenge. I had never wanted to punch the fucker in the face more than right this second.

"Then..." I pondered the thought a moment. I had a shit ton of blood on my hands, yet I couldn't devise a plan to save someone's life?

Only because you're good at taking people's lives, you dumbass.

"We lie. We protect her and ourselves, and we lie," Tuck declared.

I rang my hands together in frustration. It wasn't foolproof though, and if we got caught then we would die, maybe not us, but Ellie would and that would be the same as killing me. Now that I knew everything, I couldn't let them shed her blood because the second they did it would be an all-out war.

I would kill every single fucker that hurt her.

Starting with Drake and her father.

I would end them all, and I would smile the entire time I did it.

"I'll talk to Dex and try not to make myself a target," Tuck announced. I knew the end was coming, and I knew something bad was going to happen. I just hoped it would be after we got her out.

I had never been a praying man a day in my life, but I was praying that if I could save anyone at the end of all of this it would be her.

ELLIE

THIRTEEN

I was a wreck all day and night as I waited for Grayson to return. Every single sound had me on edge.Now that they were on the lookout for me, anything could happen. All they needed was the smallest inkling that I was here, right underneath their noses-hiding and then bam, it would all be over. All the running and hiding would be for nothing. As I sank onto Grayson's mattress, the same one that we had made passion filled memories on, I realized just how much he meant to me. It wasn't about the sex, or the fact that he wanted to help me escape.

It was that for the first time in my life someone was out to protect me from the evil in the world. What would my life had been like had Drake been the knight that Grayson is?

Don't get me wrong, I knew Grayson was evil. That he had sinned in darker ways, after all he was working as one of my father's henchmen; but it was more than that. Grayson was grey, where Drake was black. He did for the world what others refused to do.

Yet, the burning question in my mind that replayed like a never-ending song was if it came down to it, would he shoot me? Would he kill me? We had only shared a small amount of time together. What started as infatuation was going to end up burning us both. His darkness called to me, even when I knew I should've ran.

My heart was ringing in my ears as a storm brewed outside, raindrops pelted the window across the room and as much as I craved to trace those drops as they fell against the glass I didn't.

Even the smallest things like that could be seen and get me killed. A shrill laugh escaped me.

"Don't touch the windows, Ellie. It'll get you killed." Shaking that thought from my head, I picked at one of the pillows on the bed. A whiff of cologne hit me right in the nostrils. It was woodsy, mixed with smoke and rain. I brought the pillow up to my face, taking in a deeper breath of the smell, allowing it to sink deeply into my veins, calming my heartbeat and breathing.

Grayson struck fear in me, but at the same time brought me as close to heaven as I would ever get.

"Your beauty is magnificent." I heard his voice before I saw it.

A blush formed against my cheeks. "Did you find anything out?" I asked, placing the pillow against the bed sheets.

"A plan has been devised, it's not foolproof and the chance of it working out is slim to none, but so is everything you truly want in life... Kind of like you." His voice was firm but soft almost as if you could lay yourself on it and be comforted by it in the same notion.

"What do you mean?" Confusion was setting in.

"I told myself that I wouldn't care about what happened to you. That if things ended badly it wouldn't be the first time I had seen bloodshed. Except it's different with you. I was so beyond fucking wrong to think that I could taste you once and allow it to be enough. That I could let you walk away after taking you." His admission shocked the hell out of me.

What could I say to that?

"You're everything I hate, yet everything I need. You aren't supposed to be here, but I want you here. It's the most dangerous thing I have ever done, but at the same time the most exhilarating."

"I don't know what to say, Grayson, it was pure infatuation. I never meant to cause problems..." Tears formed behind my eyes. Was I truly falling for this man? For everything that I shouldn't be? Hate was such an easier emotion to feel towards someone, but I couldn't with him. Not after all he had sacrificed.

He crossed the room in the blink of an eye, one of his large hands reaching out to me, cupping my cheek. It was such a soft motion, such a delicate thing to do, but one that made me shy away from his touch. I had never known love and when you didn't know anything but pain and hurt in your life, delicate and soft wasn't something you were used to.

"I'm going to protect what is mine, Ellie." His breath fell against my cheek. "I will always protect you, even when you leave this place." My shoulders sagged and just as I was about to turn away he gripped me under the chin tipping my face upwards, pressing his lips against mine. The kiss was explosive, a mixture of emotions that I had needed to set me off.

My dam had been broken open and now a flood was about to take place. Before Grayson I was afraid of drowning, afraid of sinking to the bottom of my own lake, but now Grayson was my life vest.

The kiss deepened, and before either of us realized it clothes were being shed. He shoved me gently upon his mattress and looked down at me with misery and amazement in his eyes. It wasn't something that any other woman would understand, but I got Grayson where others wouldn't.

The sound of air filling lungs met my ears. "I want this to be what you remember about me. The passion, the way I touch you as you reach the edge of your peak." His words were so strong and full that a tear fell from my eye as I stared up at him watching his every move.

His movements were jerky as he shed his own clothing, showing off abs of steel and a V that made my mouth water. I wanted so badly to sit up and lick the crease, but instead stayed in place, my fingers digging into my palm. His eyes darkened, telling me that he wasn't playing. Everything about him at this very point said rough and powerful. "I want you. Even if I shouldn't, even if it's against all the rules, even if we both die tonight this is what I want." That was all he needed to hear and he was on me, like a moth to a flame he covered his body with my own, blanketing me in warmth and a tenderness that sank into my soul.

His lips pressed kisses against my neck, while his beard rubbed against my skin in a way that turned me on far more than it should have.

"I will miss the way you feel above me," I whispered as if it was a secret admission that I shouldn't have said. He didn't stop or even verify that he had heard me. Instead he kissed me harder, his fingers gripping my body in a bruising manner, but it didn't frighten me or even bother me. It made me feel, it reminded me that he was here.

Taking my own hands, I rubbed them down his back, scars that I hadn't noticed before marred his skin. Oh the pain he had endured, I could feel the sorrow and anger in each jagged line as my finger traced over it.

"Don't feel sorry for me," he growled, gripping me by my hair as to bring my face closer into his. His features were dark, his loving demeanor gone.

"I don't," I snarled, reaching out and biting his bottom lip just enough to draw a smear of blood. He licked at the wound, his eyes flickering between madness and completely turned on.

"Good." With a shove he released me, gripping my hips in one swift movement and pulling me to the edge of the bed. His fingers dug into my skin and it was as if someone was filling my veins with a drug that could numb all the pain, a drug that could take all the sadness away.

"Dripping for me, huh?" He licked his own lips as one of his thick digits circled my clit and entrance. Was I already soaked for him? It seemed unnatural for me, but with Grayson everything was different.

I nodded my head and a pleasing smile showed on his face right as he bent down and licked me from the top of my pussy to my ass. My thighs tensed, my legs lifting off the mattress. This time was so different, this time I allowed myself to feel everything. Every emotion, every lick, touch, and push. This time there would be no limit.

"Do you like that?" He purred against my pussy, his words causing a vibration against my clit. My body shuddered and my belly started to tingle.

"Please, more, so much more..." I begged. It wasn't hard for him to give into me, because in a moment's time he was back to where he was before, his tongue gliding at the sweetness between my legs. Every swipe of it forcing me to remember what feeling truly was.

"So good…" I squealed, grinding my pussy against his face, not getting enough of what he was giving me. Fingers dug into the inside of my thighs as he held me firmly in place giving me only what he wanted me to have.

"Stay put…" His growl sparked an avalanche inside of me. My legs shook and the butterflies in my belly released, as he sucked every drop of life out of me. Light blinded me as I gripped his head holding it in place, never wanting this moment to end even though I knew it would all too soon.

My body convulsed, and just as Grayson pulled away from me I heard the creaking of a door. Unaware of what was about to take place, I sat up and noticed just how true my previous thought was.

We were fucked.

Literally.

FOURTEEN

I should have known that rolling the dice one too many times was like playing an insane game of Russian roulette. I also should have known that only the ugliest of men attacked while another man was down, and while having Ellie lay before me spread eagle would've been one of the best ways to go out it, wasn't the last memory I wanted with her.

"Liar, liar..." Cole bellowed, his words echoing off the walls. Turning swiftly, I grabbed a sheet from the bed throwing it at Ellie and grabbing my own pants off the floor. If this fucker wanted to brawl we could, but I wasn't letting him see Ellie or myself naked.

"For there to be a lie you would have to have known that something was going on, and for every lie there is a truth, Cole," I said, my voice firm as I turned around ready to face the music. I knew they would find out eventually. I was just praying that I would have more time with her.

Cole smirked and then a sickening laugh filled the air, one that made my belly roll with disgust. "Here we all are looking for her, and all along you had her. Hiding her or protecting her neither which I care for, because you both are as good as dead."

"You don't know a damn thing," I sneered. Now was the time when I needed to put my game face on, now was the time when Ellie would look at me like she did everyone else. She had to believe at the end of all of this that all I ever wanted was to save her from the darkness, to cure the pain she had been caused.

"I know you kept this from us." His growl was loud as his eyes narrowed and the shadows of two more of the guys appeared behind him.

"The plans I devise are my own!" I yelled, I was about to blow up. I wanted to protect Ellie from them! I wanted to scream it at the top of my lungs, but I knew there was no way out now. I had to come up with something, a lie, a formulated plan that only I would understand. It would break her, but it would save her.

"Plans?" Dex stepped forward coming into the light, his eyes lingering on Ellie's image before meeting my stare.

"Yes, plans. When I discovered who she was I made plans to keep her. Since the moment I found out she was the woman we were looking for, I had to do whatever I could to make her feel comfortable. If she caught on or didn't think I cared, then she would've escaped." Every single word that left my mouth was like a stab to the chest. I could feel the room fill with uncertainty on both sides. Ellie most certainty would believe that it had all been a setup, which would lead Dex, Cole, and Luke to believe me as well.

There was indifference in Dex's eyes as he continued to analyze the situation. Ellie was still and silent, a glance over my shoulder showed just how final everything was to her. Hurt and anger showed in her blue eyes, but there was more, so much more; words that were left unsaid. Words I would never get to hear.

"Good, then you can be the one to kill her..." Cole trailed off, advancing towards the bed. He was testing me, to see if I would stop him. My muscles tensed as he grew closer, but I knew if I made the wrong move it would be the end for both of us. There would be no future for Ellie. I couldn't take that from her just because I didn't like the circumstances.

Her life matters.

Her future is her own.

I repeated the words to myself.

Cole's shoulder slammed against me in rage as he manhandled Ellie, gripping her from my bed by her dark hair.

"Leave me the fuck alone!" Ellie spat, fighting fiercely against his hold. She didn't understand that fighting just made it all worse. Cole would hurt her for her actions, and there wouldn't be a fucking thing I could do about it if I wanted to throw them off.

"Sorry, babe, but you fucked up big time with your daddy, and therefore it's our job to take care of you." Cole smirked, his fist gripping her locks of hair in a more aggressive manner. Everyone stood still as they waited to see if I would protect her.

"What? Take her, she was a good fuck while it lasted." I shrugged my shoulders, keeping my face as motionless as possible.

"Fuck you! Fuck all of you. You're all ruthless bastards... All of..." The words stopped coming the moment Cole struck her with his hand across her temple. I watched my hands, aching to catch her body as she fell to the wooden floor. I bit the inside of my cheek distracting myself from her pain, blood pooled inside of my mouth but it did no good. My eyes still stayed glued to hers as she stared at me, longing for some type of protection or answer.

"Listen, bitch, this isn't a game I want to play. Gray here fucked you good, in more than one way and now you have to deal with the consequences." Without warning, Cole gripped her by the hair again pulling her to her feet. A cry of pain left her perfectly pink lips.

"You did good, Grayson. I may have to reward you after all, I mean I was planning your funeral before, but now you made my life about ten times easier." Dex crossed the room, placing a hand upon my shoulder. I nodded, smiling at him as I watched Cole drag Ellie away.

"I hate you, Grayson!!" she yelled as loud as she could just as Cole slammed the door behind him. I didn't know where he was taking her and as my heart pounded out of my chest, I knew if I found out I would do anything I could to help her escape.

"Hate is such a strong word," Luke mumbled, stepping out the shadows. He was the silent killer. Always lurking. If I was right about things he probably noticed what was going on first.

"I'll let the boss know you found her. He will be beyond pleased with you," Dex said gleefully. My stomach twisted in knots, my throat burned with unsaid words, but what was I to do? Even if I did get her out of here now, there would be no hope for her and I.

What was infatuation had bloomed into love, and love was now on the verge of killing us both. I didn't know what to do from here on out, but I had to find a way to make sure she didn't reach her father.

"Actually…" Luke added. "Maybe we should see if he could fly out and see for himself the good deed that Grayson has done." It wasn't so much what Luke said, but how he said it that made me question everything I knew about him. He didn't seem to react to anything that was going on, yet his eyes were on Ellie the entire time.

"Yes! I agree, we could have a little welcoming party for him." Dex sounded overly excited and as I watched Luke. I knew there was something off about him.

"Do you guys have any idea where Tuck is?" I asked nonchalantly, buttoning my pants the rest of the way and grabbing my shirt off the floor.

"Nah. We aren't his keeper, but I'm sure he's out clubbing and picking up his nightly fuck." Luke laughed, his eyes burning a hole through me. I knew better than to think I had been let off this easily. They didn't believe me, and if they did they hardly did.

Whatever my next move was it needed to be quiet and precise. Ellie and I were riding on the line between life and death, and right now it looked like death had the upper hand.

ELLIE

FIFTEEN

Light blinded my eyes and my head pounded as I tossed in bed from side to side. I could feel myself floating, my body aching from every blow that I had taken the night before. My arms refused to hold my weight as I rolled over to get myself out of the bed before he awoke.

I had to leave, I had to find a way out of this mess called my life. Living under my father's thumb another moment longer was like diving into the deep end of the pool without knowing how to swim. I was drowning here, in this place. Worst of all, if I didn't get out now I would die.

What a bitch! The words smacked me in the face as much as the cold water that landed on me. I blinked my eyes open, my head aching as the coldness of the ground beneath me settled into my bones.

Confusion settled in, but soon disappeared as I looked up into a pair of a dark green eyes unknown to me. They were full of anger and vengeance. Nothing about the way he was looking at me said I was going to make it out of this alive.

How had he allowed them to take me? Grayson's words stung far more than any beating I had ever taken. I trusted him to care of me, to get me out of here. Yet, opening my eyes showed me nothing but death and pain to come.

He hadn't failed me, he killed me.

"Let me go," I muttered. I knew it was useless, and my heart hurt as the words that Grayson had said swam around my brain. Only he could make me feel wanted and hated all at the same time.

Dangerous Ties by J.L. Beck

The man before me chuckled, his laugh deep as if what he was really laughing about was something hilarious. I rolled my eyes without thought which caused him to reach out and grip me by the arm, pulling me from the floor.

"Stop touching me," I screamed, attempting to pull my arm from his hold. It did me no good though because in a second I was hit again, my head bouncing off the hard floor. Stars showed before my eyes, and I could feel a small trickle of blood dripping down my face.

"I'm in charge. I'm IN CHARGE." Spit clung to my face as the man bent down and screamed the words at me. Tears formed and began falling from my eyes, the pain in my head beating like a drum. I turned away from his voice, just wanting all of it to end.

You put yourself here, Ellie. You believed him and listened to his words. Now you have a broken heart and your own death looming in the air.

"Get the fuck up!" Another booming voice met my ears, but I held my eyes firmly closed. A kick landed against my stomach, forcing all the breath from my bottom. Pain throbbed on every inch of my flesh, but I refused to give in.

Gritting my teeth, I held the pain in.

A scream was what they wanted. They needed to know they were making a point. I couldn't let them win.

"I know you aren't dead, slut. Did you suck the cum off his dick, too?" He snickered as he kicked me again, the steel of his boot landing against my rib. A crack met my ears with the impact, causing a muffled cry to escape me.

"About time you showed something… Your daddy's about to come, and he ain't going to rescue you." I rolled away from the voice. I just wanted to die.

"Leave her to me." The voice associated with those words caused the blood in my veins to run cold. I knew that voice, the anger behind those words, and what would happen the moment I was left alone with him.

"Luke, man, you know this is my thing…" *Luke? Who was Luke?* My eyes popped open, meeting his dark ones. It was like looking the devil right in the eye and knowing he would kill you in an instant.

"Boss asked me to perform some special duties, Cole. Just here to do my job." I twisted away from both of them, the room growing darker with each passing second.

Cole raised his hands, slight irritation evident in his eyes and he stepped away, walking out of the room that I was being held in. When the door closed behind him, the door to a freedom filled life also closed.

"You've truly out done yourself, Ellie. I mean this time you've decided to not only run from me, but to fuck another man. ANOTHER man!" he screamed, his voice causing my ears to ring.

"I did nothing, Drake," I pleaded, even though I didn't want to. I wanted to be strong. I wanted to fight back, but I couldn't, there was no point in any of it. I would die at the end of all of this, all at the hands of the man I was trying to run from.

"You did. Not only are you a fucking slut, but you're a liar. A liar, Ellie, and you know what your father has me do with those that lie... You remember, right?" Drake's footfalls were heavy, each one of impending doom until he was halting right in front of me. He pulled a knife from his pocket bringing it down to my throat.

"Please..." I cried out. I was far too weak to fight him, and even if I tried it wouldn't matter. Someone else would get to me before I could escape.

Drake smiled like a snake being served his first meal in days. "Please..." He mocked me.

"Don't... Don't kill me yet..." I blinked my eyes open, staring at him in the most convincing way I could. Slowly his eyes softened, one of his hands reaching down to comb through my blood-matted hair.

"I'll do whatever you want," I pleaded with him, still unmoving because I wasn't sure what would happen next. Drake was like a ticking time bomb. If he exploded, it was all over.

Instead of doing so, he did something I least expected- he smiled, but just as fast as it appeared it vanished.

"Like your pity me eyes could ever work on me again," he sneered, his fingers digging into my hair as he pulled to lift me from the ground. My scalp burned and fresh tears fell from my eyes as a scream resonated from deep within my chest. "I know better now. I know better than to trust you. After I watched you fuck Grayson on that video. We had a camcorder in that room... bet neither of you knew that. Now, I have much better plans."

Shivers racked my body, the beating of my heart was loud in my ears as Drake slammed me against the brick wall.

"Instead..." Drake released me only to grip my chin tightly, "I'm going to fuck you until you're bleeding, until you're begging me to stop. Then, and only then will I scar your body the way you have scarred my heart by being a slut." His breath blasted against my skin as the blade slid against my throat. I could feel the sharp edge sink into my skin just enough to cause a small cut.

My flesh burned as Drake made a trail with his hand between my legs. I squeezed my eyes closed and pressed my thighs together as hard as I could.

"Do you think that will stop me?" he whispered, biting my nipple hard enough to draw blood. A scream crept out of me just as his hand attempted to pry my legs open. Something inside of me snapped and no longer could I hold on. My thighs went slack and my body flailed against the wall.

"That's my girl, take it like the slut you are. Give that pussy to me," Drake growled, his tongue licking away the blood on my throat. My mind started to close in on itself just as Drake's fingers entered me harshly. Pain formed but didn't register in my mind. I was going in on myself, burying all the hurt again.

He will come for you, Ellie.

He loves you, Ellie.

He wants you.

You're worthy. I kept telling myself, hoping every word whispered was true.

"Hey, fuckwad, if she wanted it she would be moaning by now." I didn't know that voice and the last thing I wanted was another man to come and try and hurt me. I squeezed my eyes together harder than I had before, not wanting to see the end happen. I could hear the bone meeting bone, and then the sound of a body hitting the floor. Relief soared through me as soon as I realized Drake was no longer touching me. Breath entered my lungs, and I sunk to the floor with the shadow of a man above me.

I blinked, trying to focus on him, his image, and what he was saying but my ears seemed to stop working. My body shook, the cold floor biting into my naked flesh. I had been used and abused, again and again. This time would be no different.

"I'm going to save you," the voice said, and I watched as he pulled a needle out of his pocket.

Save me? With that? How would he do that? I tried to ask him questions out loud but nothing would come out. My mouth was unmoving, my lungs barely filling with oxygen as I fought to move away from him. The fight was useless as he grabbed my arm, plunging the needle deep into my skin. A burning sensation covered my body in an instant.

I twisted my head back and forth, my body filling with panic as the feeling of control left my me and my heart rate slowed down.

"It's all going to be okay now... Everything is going to be okay." The mystery man's cool breath fell against my cheek, and it was in that coolness that I realized I had smelt that cologne before. That I'd heard that voice before.

I knew this man. I had to.

I tried to blink my eyes open more, only for them to close more firmly. I was falling deeply into the abyss. Nothing could save me now.

SIXTEEN

My senses were on high alert, my heart rate skyrocketed, and my hands felt clammy. I was wearing a suit, wining and dining with my boss when I should've been putting a gun to his head and rescuing his daughter.

Patience.

I thought I could walk into the dining area and not want to wrap my hands around his throat, but I was wrong. The second I saw his eyes I could see the resemblance to Ellie's, which only made the fire in my veins burn hotter. I was ready to fuck him up, to cause him all the same pain he had caused her. Worst yet, Tuck wasn't anywhere in sight to keep me from doing something stupid. I hadn't seen him since earlier when I went to him for advice, and none of the other guys knew where he was either. I was starting to go out of my mind, especially since he went completely off the fucking radar.

"Tonight is for you, bud!" Dex congratulated me like I had saved someone's life or something. A beer landed in my hands, and just as I brought it to my lips her father started to speak.

"Grayson…" His voice was deep and robust. He held authority when he talked and everyone seemed to be drawn to him, everyone but me.

"I hope my daughter wasn't as much trouble as she often is." He smirked, showing off perfectly straight white teeth. I had met him only a few times before, and he seemed to look the same each time. Anger ruled over everything as I stared at him; images of my dead sister's body, the fact that I knew her killer could be in this room. My mind drifted back to images of Ellie as she was beat by his men.

"No, not at all sir," I ground out between gritted teeth. I took a long chug from the beer, it took everything inside of me not to take this bottle and smash it against his head. I knew there was more behind everything, and from the way he was watching me I wondered if he was going to tell me.

"Good, good. I'm glad that it was you who found her. I know we have had quite a rocky road, but I want you to know that I still love you as if you were my son and I your father," he said sincerely. His words making the cracks in my heart more profound, and I gripped the bottle hard in my hand, waiting for the moment the glass would break.

"Thank you..." I grunted, trying not to sound as angry as I was feeling.

"You don't have to..." Boss started to say but stopped midsentence as one of his guards stepped in to whisper something in his ear. His eyes grew wide with a mix of emotions, first fear and then anger. He gripped his tie, tightly adjusting it before speaking again.

"Men, I hate to cut this celebration short as we can always come back and celebrate, but I need you back at the house with me." Fear rooted me in place. What had his bodyguard said, and why did we need to go back to the house? If we went back to the house we would see Ellie, and that meant she would be killed before I ever got my hands on her.

"What's going on, boss?" Dex asked, concerned. His dark eyes peering into my own as if it was I who had done something wrong.

Cole was lounging in the corner by the bar watching and waiting for the next victim, completely oblivious to what was taking place.

"It's been discovered that my daughter is finally dead..." Boss smiled, and my heart sank into my stomach. Emotions flooded me at every angle. She couldn't be dead... there was no way, who had killed her?

"What happened?" I blurted out without cause, if she was dead what was the purpose of hiding my feelings anymore? Dex shot me a dirty look as if to say my loud voice and question asking hadn't gone unnoticed.

The rest of the boss' men gathered around, including Cole who was supposed to be with Ellie. My mind wandered through people slowly as I tried to figure out who it was that should've been watching over her.

"What the fuck happened? I left her with Luke and now she's dead? Did Luke kill her? I mean nothing against you, boss, but the bitch is annoying as fuck. I would've killed her eventually as well," Cole added.

"Luke? Is he okay?" Dex jumped in. Boss watched us all closely, pulling his phone from his pocket.

"The limo is waiting out front to take us back. We need to find out what happened, and then I will enlighten you all." Boss smiled down at his phone, his beady little eyes showing deadly secrets.

In that moment I prayed as hard as I could that Ellie was still alive. That once I got there it would all be seen as a mistake and Tuck would have shown back up and we could get her out of there. Even if it meant betraying them and being put on their kill list.

My feet were heavy as I lagged behind, and Cole scurried past me but not before exchanging words.

"I know you're hiding something. You fucked her without fault, Gray." I rolled my eyes, trying not to anger myself any further. I was on the edge of losing it at this very moment.

"I have nothing to explain to you, asshole," I mumbled back just as we pushed through the doors leading out to the limo. I was jittery with fear the entire drive, and as we pulled up I could feel the blood leaving my face.

God let her be alive. I will never ask for anything else in my life, but please don't let me fail another person. Please don't let this be the end.

We entered the building heading straight to the basement-in the interrogation rooms, which is where I thought they were holding her. My nerves were on edge, my heart beating in my ears as we entered the room.

Her naked lifeless body laid on the floor while Luke sat in the corner of the room, a large black and blue mark across his forehead.

"What the fuck happened?" Words were leaving my throat without thought. All my emotions were gone. Every single shred of hope had left my body as I watched her father place his fingers against her pulse.

Her skin was pale, covered in bruises and blood. Fuck! Fuck! Fuck! I had failed her, just like I had failed my sister, Stephanie. I failed them all... and for what?

"She's gone," Boss announced, and it was then that I completely lost my shit. My fists were flying without a moment's notice, my hands shaking. I punched the nearest wall, causing all the attention to be brought on me.

"She better be gone. Bitch caused more damage than anything." Luke's voice was hoarse as if he had been yelling for hours. Boss looked at me and then down to my bleeding fist.

"What's a matter, son?" He paused before looking back at Luke.

"Seems to me that there were other things that weren't brought to my attention?" he added, before I could answer. I hadn't thought before acting, but then again what was the fucking point. The whole reason for me to live was lying lifelessly on the floor, and worst of all was that her death now weighed on my shoulders.

I had killed the woman I loved, and I hadn't even been the one to take her last breath away. *Love?* Had that singular word escaped me. I knew it hadn't been that long since I've known her, but I felt for her what I had never felt for others. So was it love? My eyes burned, and my breath felt like it was stuck in my chest. It was more than love, it was compassion and fear for someone that I hadn't been able to tell I loved. All I wanted to do was lay on the floor next to Ellie and hold her for as long as I could. I wanted to bring her back even if just for a second to tell her how I feel, and how sorry I was to have failed her.

"I just..." I growled. "I thought I was going to have the chance to end her life." I lied. I still needed answers. I would get them. I would avenge for not only my sister, but for Ellie too. I would bring this man to his knees and beat him into the ground. I would become the secret killer he never saw coming.

Dangerous Ties by J.L. Beck

"No need to feel bad, at least she's dead," Dex added. My nails dug into my palm. Blood poured from the wound on my fist, but I didn't care.

"I have some news I wanted to let you guys in on. I thought at least there would be one snake in this group, but I guessed wrong. I had a man very close to me undercover in the group staying with you," Boss spoke loudly. As shocking as this news was it wasn't that shocking; at least not until he added the last part.

"The undercover boss was Luke, who is actually my son in law. His real name is not Luke, but Drake." Boss smiled wide and happy as if he had granted us the biggest secret of all. I looked straight into Drake's ugly fucking face, a million and one different emotions raging a war inside of me.

This man had hurt my Ellie, this man had done horrible things to her, and he was going to pay.   Now   everyone would pay.

I would end everyone's life, simply to bring life back to her.

TO
BE
CONTINUED

Loved it? Hated it? Tell us about it. Leave a review on Amazon today and make your opinion count.

Made in the USA
Middletown, DE
07 March 2016